PERFECT TIMING

A.D. ELLIS

AUTHOR'S NOTE

Note about demisexuality: First, and foremost, the term demisexual can mean different things for different people. Charlie is a unique individual, just like the rest of us, and the way demisexuality works for him may not be the way it works for others.

For more information regarding demisexuality, please see the articles HERE and HERE.

If you don't have time to check the articles, I pulled out a couple quotes I think are helpful (but I'd still encourage you to read and learn for yourself).

"Demisexuality is a sexual orientation where people only experience sexual attraction to folks that they have close emotional connections with."

"Again, every person is unique, and what one demisexual person enjoys might not be what another person enjoys."

ONE

CHARLIE HILLION

"CHARLIE! This damn TV isn't working and I've got a program to watch. While you're at it, bring me a cocktail and my porn collection." Uncle Otto's words crackled over the baby monitor we'd set up.

I chuckled at the cantankerous old man's demands. "Be there in a bit," I said into the device on my kitchen counter. "Someone is grumpy today," I said to my cats, Cricket and Hopper, as they watched me from their perches on the back of the couch.

Otto would be itching to watch *Days of Our Lives* and all hell would break loose if he missed the opening scene. He'd nap during the next show and wake in time to watch reruns of *Judge Judy*.

I gathered his afternoon medication and sent up a heartfelt prayer of gratefulness we'd been able to secure a home health nurse to start soon. I had no problem caring for Otto, but I wasn't a trained medical professional and it worried me I'd screw something up.

Otto was the only family I had left. My mother had died when I was young. My father, Otto's brother, Orson, had passed away recently which was why Otto and I were now cohabitating. Orson had been Otto's caregiver, but he hadn't given two shits about his own son.

At forty-five, I'd been estranged from my father for over two decades. Imagine my shock when he left me everything he had upon his death. The only stipulation was I had to make sure Otto was cared for.

"Be good while I'm gone, boys," I told my cats. They yawned and went back to sunning themselves.

With a glass of orange juice—complete with the fancy umbrella decoration Otto insisted on—medication, and a crossword puzzle book written in large font, I headed out of the main house to the tiny guest house cottage out back.

I adored my new yard. The deck was only a couple years old and got amazing shade for a good portion of the day. The path between my house and Otto's place was paved with flat rocks and lined with gorgeous peony bushes. The trees were mature and had recently been trimmed to keep the roofs safe from falling limbs.

Pausing just long enough to admire one of the three large flower beds, I mentally planned what types of flowers I could maybe plant for next year. As I glanced toward the lilac bush, I thought ahead to the little fish pond and fountain I wanted to add in the near future.

Leaving the respite of the yard—after years in the city, having my own little chunk of nature was a needed boost for my mental health—I made my way to Otto's place and walked on in.

"Put that shit down and get this damn TV working," Otto barked from his recliner. He wasn't a mean man, just had no filter and got a little twitchy if he missed his programs. I'd finally convinced him we could record them to watch later if needed, but he still preferred watching at the scheduled time.

I took the remote from him and checked the batteries

first. He had a bad habit of borrowing batteries from one device to use in another. "You took the batteries out."

"My dildo was dead," he quipped.

I snorted. While I didn't doubt he had a dildo—the man was very open and I'd heard way too much about his sex life, both independent and partnered—I knew I'd *just* given him batteries for that last week. "No way you've used that thing so much it's dead again. If you have, I better get you to the doctor for some cream before you give yourself a friction burn."

Otto cracked up. "Nah, my razor was dead. Get some batteries from the baby radio."

I chuckled. "Nope, that's off limits remember? We don't borrow batteries from that. Ever."

"You've got about two minutes to get my program on before I start telling you about the time I walked in on your dad beatin' off while watching *The Three Stooges*."

"Oh God, stop." Otto and Orson had gotten along fine, but they were about as different as night and day. Orson had a soft spot for his brother and accepted Otto's differences. Which was always a slap in the face when he couldn't accept I definitely marched to the beat of my own drummer. Maybe he felt his *son* being weird was more a reflection on him than his brother being different.

I grabbed new batteries from the drawer and put them in the remote. Turning the TV to *Days of Our Lives*, I settled in to watch the first scene with Otto. There was no way I'd get him to take his medication while the show was on.

Otto's home was perfect for him. Sparsely furnished as to not become a hazard for him moving around, but decorated with many of his favorite pieces from his past. He was an eclectic man and his house portrayed that.

A few minutes later, as the opening credits played, I nudged the OJ toward him and held out the pills. "Drink up.

And don't forget we're going for a walk. Doctor wants you getting movement so those joints don't stiffen up."

"Speaking of stiffen up, did you bring my porn?"

I sighed. "I set it up on your laptop, remember? You don't even have to login or anything. Double click the icon and it should take you right to your account." I couldn't believe I'd set my eighty-year-old uncle up with porn account. But my father had been very specific that I used some of the money he'd left me to take care of the man, and Otto swore porn kept him young and energetic. Plus, it was better than trying to store magazines or physical videos.

"What's an icon?"

"A picture. Take your pills." I held the pills out again.

"Oh yeah, you wouldn't let me pick a dick picture so it's a banana. I remember it now. And I can watch anything I want?" He took the pills and studied them.

"Yep, I set your favorites so it should automatically show the categories you picked." Otto would have likely been the poster child for *pansexual* if the label had been around back in his day. To hear him tell it, he'd slept with any and every pretty thing he'd had the opportunity to back then. The same was true now days, he just didn't have as many opportunities.

I envied my uncle being so open and easy and certain when it came to who he was attracted to and who he had sex with. I was *definitely* not like him in that aspect. Well, I knew who I was attracted to and I knew who I wanted to have sex with, but everything got murky beyond that.

Otto scowled as he swallowed his pills. "This cocktail is severely lacking vodka. Don't think I can't tell."

"You can't drink vodka with your medicine. Might as well accept your only option now is to be drunk on life." I took the empty glass from him and smiled as he slipped the paper umbrella behind his ear like a flower.

"Might as well tell me to curl up and die," Otto groused. "We don't have to walk. I know you have work to do." He waved a hand as if dismissing me.

"No way, no how. You watch your shows and I'll work. Then we'll walk to that little coffee shop. Maybe eat dinner there if you want." I checked to be sure the baby monitor was placed up high enough Otto couldn't steal its batteries and tossed a blanket on his lap. "I'll come get you a little later. Holler if you need me."

The soap opera was back on so all I got was a little wave. The man had been watching the show for longer than I'd been alive and he was obsessed. I smiled to myself as I left the little cottage and headed to the main house.

When Orson died and I found out he'd left me a shit ton of money, my first thought was Otto. They'd been living in Indianapolis because my dad preferred the city. But Otto had quickly demanded a move to a small town when I'd asked what he wanted to do. We found a house for sale in the tiny town of Briarton and the rest was history.

While I didn't *have* to take over caring for Otto, I was happy to do it. I loved the old man in a way I hadn't ever been able to love my own father. Probably because Otto accepted me for who I was and didn't seem ashamed of me. Guilt often plagued me because I would have been a lot more upset to lose Otto than my father.

My job as a writer could be done from anywhere and Briarton was a perfect little town. The house's former owner, Harley Wade, had sold because he was moving in with his girlfriend. At first, I'd insisted Otto have the main house; I could easily make-do in the smaller cottage-like guest house, but he refused.

"I don't get around as well as I used to. No use living somewhere with stairs when I won't be able to use them. I can visit the main house, you can visit the guest house. We'll have our own space and privacy when it's needed." He'd winked and pointed to the baby monitor. "I'll turn it off if I'm about to get busy."

I'd laughed and shook my head. "Nope. That's untouchable. First, who you getting busy with? Second, if I hear something I don't want to hear, I'll turn it down on my end. Three minutes will probably be enough time," I'd teased.

"There are quite a few attractive people in this town," Otto had said. "Never know when I might romance one of them into my bed." He shrugged. "Or maybe you'll just hear me on a date with Dave."

"Dave?"

"My dildo," he'd said with a wicked grin. "Or maybe Jack."

I'd rolled my eyes. "Do I even want to know?"

"Fleshlight," Otto had quipped.

If the man was getting as much action as he talked about it, I didn't know how he had time for anything else.

I enjoyed a leisurely walk through the yard as I headed back to my place. As a writer, I had to be sure I didn't spend my entire day sitting or my brain—and body—would atrophy into something completely unusable. Getting out for some sunshine and fresh air was always part of my daily schedule.

Before heading up to my office, I called to Cricket and Hopper and played with them for several minutes. After a few good pounces and romping around with each other, they both gave me their blessing for belly rubs and then demanded treats. As my boys happily devoured their snack, I grabbed a water and went upstairs to get some words down.

By late afternoon, I'd finished up the final touches on a manuscript I'd been writing. I always had several projects going at once, but I liked it that way because it kept me busy. Staying busy was a blessing and a curse. It meant I always had a good reason not to go out, socialize, make friends, leave my safe little burrow. But it also meant I had an excuse not to go out, socialize, make friends, leave my safe little burrow. I did love writing and it was a good job, it just didn't lend itself to a lot of people-ing.

The current work in progress was under my ghostwriter name. I hoped to finish a mystery novel under another name within a week or two—I'd send that one off to the publisher and let them take it from there. I also had four content articles due within a few days, but I could bang those out no problem. The romantic comedy I'd been working on for months under my self-published pen name—the book I was the most passionate about—was taking longer and giving me fits. I was ready for it to see the world, but it was nowhere close to finished.

My best friend and former roommate, Stella—she'd decided to travel the world and find herself shortly before Orson died—had been on me to write a romance ever since we'd met, saying it would allow me to create the stories I wanted for myself and maybe give me the boost I needed to make those stories happen.

Stella was a force to be reckoned with and meeting her had truly changed my life for the better. Over ten years ago, after I had a bit of a health wake-up call and forced myself to go to the gym despite my social anxieties, Stella and I had both been huffing and puffing on the treadmills.

Extrovert extraordinaire that she was, Stella had somehow swept me into conversation—she did most of the talking—and we ended up at lunch. I truly believed she was a godsend way back then because we were both in need of a roommate. We moved in together and spent a decade happily cohabitating.

She was the first and only person I would have ever called a true friend. I had acquaintances, but it was hard for me to make connections and build lasting relationships. Stella and I just clicked. We likely would have ended up being more if either of us found ourselves attracted to the opposite sex.

Stella had been the one to help me come to terms with being gay. I'd known, deep down, for years and years, but I wasn't the type to date or go to parties, so it wasn't really something I ever talked about. Once it was out in the open with Stella, and as our friendship progressed, I was able to voice other things. Like how I could find a handful of attractive men just walking a block around our apartment, but have no inclination to sleep with them. Or the fact I liked gay porn and I got myself off often, but the thought of sex with a stranger completely turned me off.

I *wanted* sex. I was attracted to men. But thinking about random hookups with men I didn't know was enough to send me running for the hills.

Over the years, Stella and I had finally worked out I was a gay, demisexual man. I was attracted to men, but my desire to have sex with those men was next to nothing unless I was able to get to know them and form a strong emotional bond.

And that was something very unlikely to happen.

I was close with Stella and Otto. That was about it.

"It's not that you *can't* make friends," Stella had said. "Friendship with you has to be coaxed and nurtured. You don't go out much. If you do, you aren't the type to strike up a conversation. Your job allows you to stay home. When you get out for exercise or food, you do what you set out to do and get back to work. You're not the type who seeks out conversation and that's okay, but it makes it hard to make connections. Without connections, your sex drive is like *Nah, I'm good*."

So, there I was in a new little town, living with my ornery uncle, writing whatever I needed to write in order to pay the bills and keep my mind free of a mishmash of thoughts, and preparing for another decade of loneliness.

And wasn't that just the shit of it all. I didn't want or need a lot of friends. I'd been perfectly happy with Stella—and missed the hell out of her—but our relationship didn't do anything for me sexually. I liked sex—well, I liked getting off and I liked the idea of sex with someone else—it was just the actual act of getting naked and climbing into bed with someone I barely knew was hard to imagine. And I barely knew most of my acquaintances. I didn't invite people to lunch or out for drinks or walks in the park because I was perfectly happy with my words and my own company.

Until I wasn't.

The loneliness hit hard—and had hit a lot harder than normal lately. It was such a mixed bag. I needed to feel a connection in order to have sex, but making connections seemed almost impossible for me.

And that was when the heaviness would blanket me. I was forty-five damn years old, facing the reality that my life was likely nearing half over and what did I have to show for it? A few books, a bunch of ghostwriter shit I'd never get credit for, about a million articles about ridiculous crap, a best friend who left me, an uncle who was getting more sex than me, and a big ol' house where I was free to putter around for the rest of my lonely existence.

Okay, that wasn't quite fair to Stella. She needed to get out there and figure some things out for herself. I heard from her often and it sounded like she was having an amazing time. I was happy for her even though I missed her.

My life was just such a conundrum. I dreamed of having a loving relationship with the man of my dreams. But when I tried to think about meeting the man of my dreams, my brain would fill with anxiety and short-circuit. How would I ever meet someone to build a connection with if trying to meet people set me on edge?

With my head spinning and my heart aching, I gave Cricket and Hopper some love and headed back toward the cottage to get Otto for our walk. Truly, I was happy with my life most of the time. I'd always known I was different—and my father never let me forget it. He'd talk about how much he loved and missed my mom and how my quirks were so very much like hers. How did he love her so much and have so much contempt for me? Orson was the type of man to think quirky uniqueness was attractive and charming in his wife but completely off-putting and unacceptable in his son. And he let me know I was a let-down. I'd barely known my mother before she died and I spent most of my time with Uncle Otto growing up—partly because my dad didn't want me around and partly because he was gone a lot on business trips. Otto took me in and accepted the real me before I even figured out who the real me was.

At least these days I actually felt as if I knew myself. I even mostly liked myself. I was just me. Charlie Hillion. Deep down, I really did think I probably had something for others to love—I mean, Stella and Otto loved me, but I didn't know if anyone would ever actually want to spend enough time getting to know me and finally digging deep enough to find out who I was.

"'Bout time you got here, I'm hungry. Let's drive." Otto shuffled toward the door.

"Nope, we're walking. Good for both of us. And the doctor insists you get movement. The coffee shop isn't far." I held the door open for him to walk onto the porch. Hovering next to him, not wanting to smother him but knowing he sometimes needed help on the steps, we made our way down to the sidewalk. "What do you think about putting a ramp in so you don't have to mess with the steps?"

We reached the sidewalk and headed toward Piping Hot.

"Stairs are a bitch, that's for sure. Don't take them out, but adding a ramp might be helpful on days when the old knees aren't working as well as they should."

Overall, Otto was in great health. His doctor back in Indianapolis, Dr. Sallie, had been one of the reasons we looked to buy in Briarton. Dr. Sallie had known Otto wanted a small town and suggested an old acquaintance of his in Briarton.

Dr. Pierce was very friendly and welcomed us as patients. He was great with cantankerous Otto and told him how impressed he was that Otto had only recently started dealing with mobility issues.

My uncle moved pretty well once he got going so keeping him moving on a daily basis was important. Plus, getting activity and fresh air was good for me as well.

We walked the tree and flower lined sidewalks of Briarton, enjoying the early summer sun and soft breeze.

"Good place we found here," Otto said.

"I like it. Easy, friendly, pretty. It has everything we need."

Briarton really was a fantastic little town. Friendly people, beautiful homes, great local businesses, and an overall feeling of *you're welcome here*.

"You see someone was moving into the house behind us?" Otto asked.

"Yeah? We'll have to meet our new backdoor neighbor. Maybe take them a pie or something." Going over to meet a new neighbor was truly the very last thing I'd ever *naturally* want to do, but I tried to stretch my boundaries here and there. Plus, I knew Otto loved meeting new people.

Otto snorted. "I just bet you'd like to meet your backdoor neighbor. More like you'd like to have a backdoor visitor," he joked.

I rolled my eyes. "Don't be crass." Otto knew I was gay

and demisexual and had no problem with it, but he often encouraged me to get out and meet people. He was a social butterfly so it was hard for him to grasp how much I didn't *need* to chat with strangers.

"If you chatted with strangers they might become friends and then friends can sometimes turn into something more." Otto had said the words many times before.

He was right. And sometimes I did put more effort into trying to get to know someone, but I never seemed to find anyone who was willing to work at getting to know me.

Otto chuckled. "I think this place will be good for us. They all seem like good people and I can feel it in these old bones, this is going to be the jackpot for you."

"I didn't know I was playing the lottery," I said with a smirk.

"Yep, and you're going to win big. I just know it. I think this is where you'll meet the love of your life." Otto took my hand and squeezed. "Promise me you'll be open to it? I'm not saying force anything and if it doesn't feel right, let it go. But be willing to meet people, chat a bit, see where things go. You've been in a much bigger city all your life. Things are faster there. Briarton feels so comfortable and easy, a slower pace. Maybe *the one* is here and just waiting to take his time getting to know you."

"From your lips to God's ears," I said, returning his hand squeeze. But really, if I couldn't meet someone in a big city of thousands, how would I meet someone in a tiny little town? "For now, let's get some coffee and food." I pulled the door open and the little bell tinkled as we walked into the coffee shop.

"Welcome to Piping Hot," the man behind the counter said with a friendly smile. He looked to be about my age and I felt like I'd seen him a few times since we moved to town just over a week ago.

The coffee shop was actually more than just coffee. Baked goods, sandwiches, soups, coffee, tea, and smoothies were on the menu. They also had a little wine corner where they sold local wines. One of the best parts of Piping Hot was they offered use of their space for crafters, book clubs, gamers, and such.

As I glanced around the warm, comforting area, I saw three people knitting, a table of four playing some sort of card game, and a woman with a book walking toward a small alcove where three others were waiting with the same book and steaming mugs of coffee.

The coffee shop was abuzz with locals eating, drinking, visiting, and enjoying their time. I'd known within moments of my first time in the place it was a mainstay in the small town.

"Otto, Charlie, so very nice to see you. Place your order and come sit with us, please." A lady I recognized as Harley Wade's girlfriend, Jo Ellen, waved to us, bracelets jangling on her wrist.

"You okay with that?" Otto asked as we stepped to the counter.

"Yes," I said. I'd met Harley and Jo Ellen when we bought the house. They were good, kind people and I felt comfortable around them. Plus, I knew Otto would take control of the conversation.

"What can I get you?" the man behind the counter asked.

Morgan was on his name tag and I recalled he was married to Harley's grandson, Justin. They owned Piping Hot.

A strange little thrill went through me. I'd always wanted to own my own small business. I wasn't sure exactly *what*, but it sounded like fun.

"I'll have today's coffee blend, the turkey and swiss, and one of those scones," I said before turning to Otto. What I *really* wanted was a coffee with three creams, three sugars, one pump vanilla like I sometimes made at home, but I always chickened out to order the concoction in public.

I was a grown man, I should be able to order my coffee any damn way I wanted it. Justin and Morgan definitely didn't seem like the type to judge a person based on their coffee order.

Making up my mind, I decided the next time I was placing an order, I'd challenge myself to get exactly what I wanted.

"Same coffee for me. Chicken salad," Otto said as he studied the baked goods. "And that blueberry muffin, please." He elbowed me. "We should take some cookies home. The macarons."

I smiled and paid for our order. "Sure thing. Maybe get some loose-leaf tea, too. We can have an evening treat."

"We'll bring your order out," Morgan said just as his very attractive and much younger husband came around the corner.

His apron was covered in flour and I didn't miss the gentle way Morgan wiped a streak of flour from Justin's face. My heart clenched. I wanted that—that level of comfortable, easy intimacy and genuinely liking each other.

I wondered how the two men had met.

Otto and I made our way to the back-corner table where Harley and Jo Ellen sat with mugs and some kind of dessert.

Otto took a seat next to Jo Ellen and leaned over to peer at her dessert. "I don't know what it is, but it looks fun and delicious."

Jo Ellen smiled broadly. "It's so good. Justin's idea. He still makes cupcakes from time-to-time, but he also started making these *cake cups*. He chunks up cake into a cup and layers in icing. No need to slice cake, just get a cake cup."

"She might be as proud of my grandson as I am," Harley said with a wink. "But I'm partial to the cinnamon Bundt cake he makes. There's seriously nothing here that isn't good."

"Awww, thanks," Justin said with a grin as he and Morgan walked up to the table with trays and delivered our food. "We'll be back in a bit, the evening shifts are coming in so they'll take over. Anyone need anything when we come back?"

"I'd take more coffee," Harley lifted his empty mug.

"Well, how are you two finding our quaint little town?" Jo Ellen asked.

"Jo, let them eat before you start grilling them," Harley admonished.

Otto waved away the comment. "I can multitask, I have a *very* talented mouth." He winked and took a sip of coffee while Jo Ellen and Harley chuckled. "We really like the place. We haven't been all over town just yet, but the people are friendly and so far, we've found everything we need is nearby."

"That's what we love about our town. We've all worked very hard to make sure folks never *have* to leave town for their needs. Doctor, dentist, grocery, coffee and tea, bakery, food, wine, crafts, hair stylist, clothing, we pretty much have it all and I plan to keep it that way." Jo tucked a chunk of fly-away hair behind her ear with a nod. "As long as I'm alive and kickin', Briarton folks won't *need* to go out of town for anything."

"Well, except for school, but that's just the way the district is laid out," Harley added.

"How's the food?" Justin asked as he and Morgan joined us with a refill for Harley and their own mugs of what appeared to be tea.

"Excellent," I said. I wasn't rude, I could hold a conversation when needed. Mostly. I just freaked out if I thought I needed to start and maintain the conversation. And heaven help me if the other person didn't seem interested—I went into a tailspin. "Coffee is amazing, too. I may have to make a pit stop here every morning before work."

Justin beamed. "Thanks. We're proud of roasting and grinding our own beans." He took a sip of his tea. "Where is it you work? We don't have a drive-thru yet—it's in the works, but we've launched an app so you can order ahead of time."

"Oh," I said, my cheeks heating, "I, um, I work from home."

"He's a writer. Works on a lot of different things. Mystery, romance, non-fiction, and a whole host of other things." Otto smiled at me over his coffee mug. He was always my biggest cheerleader and support.

"That's awesome," Justin said. "Would we have read any of your work?"

I shook my head. "Most of what I write is as a ghostwriter and I usually don't even know who the author is; the ones I do know, I'm not allowed to say." I smirked at the impressed looks around the table. "I've written a couple mysteries under a pen name."

"He's working on a romantic comedy right now. I got to read the synopsis and it sounds great. Two guys meet and fall in love as they overcome some hilarious obstacles. I'll definitely read it." Otto cut his muffin in half.

"That's amazing," Morgan said. "I don't think I've ever met an author. I want to read your work for sure."

I chuckled. "That's kinda like asking me to parade in front of you naked. It's really hard to *know* people who read your work."

"I'll read in secret," Morgan said with a wink.

I bit into my scone and groaned. "Damn, this is good."

"Nothing bad here," Harley repeated.

"How long have you two owned this place?" Otto asked.

Justin and Morgan launched into a tale of how they met and came to own Piping Hot. It was a great story and made me realize once again just how badly I wanted what they had.

As we all laughed about Justin and Morgan's second wedding, Harley changed the subject. "Otto, you're seeing Dr. Pierce, right? We both go to him. What do you think?"

"As far as doctors go, he's pretty much likable. No complaints." Otto finished off his muffin. "Don't forget we're taking home cookies and tea," he said, elbowing me before he continued speaking to Harley. "The real question is what's this damn home health nurse going to be like. Better not come in and start messing up my routine. He starts in a couple weeks and I'm just not too sure what to think; at least I've had time to settle in before he comes in and messes up my routine."

I groaned. "Your home health nurse is going to *take care of you*."

"Oh! I didn't know you were going to be in the care of Nixon," Jo Ellen exclaimed. "He's new in town, just got here about a month ago. He's actually moving in right behind you. He's already started making visits to a few of my friends and they have nothing but amazing things to say about him."

"Well, I sure hope he's cute. It'll make the anal exams a lot more fun," Otto groused.

I groaned again as everyone else laughed.

I sure hoped this nurse, Nixon, had a lot of patience and a good sense of humor.

TWO
NIXON RILEY

"WELL, Ms. Molly, it looks like your blood pressure is good and your sugars are right where they should be." I wrapped up the blood pressure cuff and put it in my bag. After signing off on Molly's daily sugar journal, I put it back next to her chair. "You're doing a great job of keeping your measurements recorded. Don't forget to write down what you're eating. You care if I hang out just long enough to make my notes?" I held up the notebook where I'd write down everything I'd done while visiting Molly, scan it, and send a copy to her daughter who saved it in a file for future reference. I'd also send them to Dr. Pierce so we could discuss Molly's health when we met twice a week.

"You do what you need to do, Nix. You know I like having visitors," Molly patted my hand.

I took a few moments to make my notes before scanning, sending, and packing up. I checked my watch. I always tried to plan for at least a few minutes of chit chat with my clients. "I've got a bit before I need to be at my next stop."

"Perfect. I always love a good chat. Now, how are you liking Briarton?"

"It's lovely," I answered honestly. "I'll be glad to get moved into my new house. Staying in the backroom at Dr. Pierce's was helpful, but I'm glad to have my own space."

"Oh, and you got such a great house. The Werklys were great people and had several good years in that house, but I'm glad they were able to move to Florida to be closer to their grandchildren." Molly sipped the tea I'd made for her. "And your backyard neighbors are also new to town. I'm sure you all will settle in just wonderfully."

"The whole town has been really welcoming, I'm glad to be here." It was the truth. I'd escaped a highly conservative political family when I was thirty—after years of being made to hide myself in a closet. My parents and siblings, even my grandparents, *said* they loved me no matter what, but their actions said something completely different throughout the years after they knew I was gay.

My family expected me to play a part and join them in politics. From the moment I came out until the moment I finally blew up and took a stand for myself, I was miserable. I had my family persona, my public persona, and the person I actually was, but that man had to be hidden.

Thanks to my family insisting I keep my sexuality *discreet*, I found myself involved in a lot of random, meaningless, and often highly disappointing sexual encounters. I couldn't ever expect to have an actual boyfriend and no man wants to be a dirty little secret.

My family was never okay with me becoming a nurse. They constantly wanted to know why I didn't do the smart, honorable thing and become a doctor. No matter how successful I was over the years—from the emergency room, to oncology, to a prestigious doctor's office, to specializing in geriatrics, none of it was ever good enough because having a big, strapping, *gay* son who was *just* a nurse was just too much for them.

I told them I couldn't keep living a lie, I'd never join them in politics, and I needed to escape the toxic situation I'd been in ever since my teen years. I moved away from them, started working in geriatrics at a large hospital a few states away, and never looked back.

Now, at forty-five, after being a home health care nurse for five years, I'd taken a leap and accepted a job in tiny Briarton in the middle of the Midwest. I'd been working with Dr. Pierce for a month and already had a great caseload of patients.

My past was filled with meaningless, painful, and often devastating hookups that were *never* going to lead anywhere. All I wanted was a serious, committed relationship. But most guys saw me as this big, beefy, dumbfuck who was only good for sex. No one took the time to get to know me, no one wanted a soft-spoken sweet guy. When they found out I wasn't some tough guy top, they split.

Don't get me wrong, I was vers so top or bottom was good with me, but being stereotyped into being a strict top just because I looked a certain part was annoying as hell.

I was the type of guy who loved to help others. I liked being needed and appreciated. Looking back on all of my wasted years, I wondered if I'd lost the chance for a meaningful relationship. Maybe I should have just been happy with my new location, my cats, and hopefully some new friends.

"Did you bring any pictures of your cats?" Molly asked.

"Of course, I'm like a proud parent with those two," I said with a smile as I pulled out my phone and pulled up my latest pictures of my two babies.

"Now, tell me their names again?" Molly asked as she cooed over the pictures. She forgot every time I told her.

"The yellow and white one is CoJack. The more orange-yellow one is Cheddar." I'd had the boys for a few years and I couldn't imagine life without them.

"I know you're going to need to go, but please be sure to bring more pictures next time." Molly took another drink of her tea. "Can you take this to the sink? I think I'm going to take a nap before my bridge group comes over."

"Sounds like a great plan. I'll see you in a couple days. Keep up the good work." I dropped her mug off in the kitchen and hefted my bag onto my shoulder.

I had a bit of a break before I needed to be at my next patient's house—truly, I *could* have stayed longer with Molly, but I tried to keep my visits to the regularly scheduled time slots so it didn't look as if I was giving one patient preferred treatment over another.

Figuring I could stop for a coffee and lunch before my next appointment, I rounded the corner for Piping Hot. I needed to see Ms. Lydia in the early afternoon and I'd slotted a double appointment to meet my newest patient.

"Morning, Nix," Justin said with a smile from behind the counter when it was my turn to place my order. "Don't forget, you can skip the line if you use the online ordering app."

I grinned and shrugged. "Didn't know for sure I was coming in. Looks busy."

Justin beamed. "Just the way we like it. Lunch rush is always hoppin'. What can I get ya?"

"Large house roast, three creams, three sugars, one pump vanilla, and a croissant, please."

"Why don't you just get a vanilla latte?" Justin grinned as he entered the order.

"My concoction is better," I said with a shrug and swiped my card.

"Whatever you say. I'll have it up in a minute."

I moved to the pickup counter to wait while I scanned my

phone. A few messages from friends I'd said goodbye to when I moved, an appointment reminder to meet with Dr. Pierce, and a notification about a video on Twitter. Nothing terribly interesting.

I pulled up the movie app; I liked to go watch movies. Actually, I liked to go to movies, the theater, bars, sporting events, and a whole host of other entertainment venues. But doing those things alone was a real downer.

Deciding there was really nothing worth going to the movie theater for, I closed the app just as the girl behind the counter called out, "Large house roast, three creams, three sugars, one pump of vanilla."

I slipped my phone into my pocket and stepped forward, reaching for my drink just as warm fingers brushed my own. I jerked back in surprise and looked at the man reaching for my drink. "Oh, sorry. Think that one's mine."

"Sorry," the man said quietly. "Thought I was the only one with that order."

I glanced at the cup and noticed *Charlie* written on the side. Well, shit.

"Wow, my bad. That's my order, but I'm not Charlie." I gestured toward the cup. "Wise order, by the way."

The man blushed and I had the sudden urge to step close and wrap him in a warm hug.

"Thanks."

"Does Justin try to get you to change it to a vanilla latte?" I asked, reaching for my croissant the girl placed on the counter.

"Yep. I've only been in town a while, but ever since I started ordering this drink, he tries to sell me on the vanilla latte." The man's eyes sparkled as he gathered his drink.

"Large house roast, three creams, three sugars, one pump of vanilla," the girl called again.

"Ah, *this* one must be mine," I said, checking for my name on the cup.

We both turned from the counter at the same time and froze. I surveyed the crowded shop. One tiny table in a far corner. Two chairs.

I didn't *have* to drink my coffee inside, but I wasn't going to pass up the chance for a good chat with a hot guy. "Wanna share that table?"

Charlie looked as if he'd rather have an appendectomy without anesthesia, but he took a deep breath and gave a little nod.

Weird. I didn't *think* I came off as an ax murderer or anything of the sort.

We made our way to the table and sat down.

"I'm Nixon by the way," I said and held out my hand.

Charlie shook my hand and I had to fight the urge to keep his hand in mine well after the appropriate amount of time for hand-shaking. The warmth of his soft skin sent a jolt of electricity through me.

Get ahold of yourself, Nix. You meet one sexy man in your new little town and you're automatically getting ideas.

Yeah, but *look* at the guy. Who wouldn't get ideas? Dark eyes, dark hair—a touch of silver gathering at his temples. He was gorgeous and *definitely* my type.

"Charlie," he replied, gesturing to the name on his cup. "Are you the Nixon who does home health nursing?"

"The one and the same," I answered, grinning broadly. I loved my job and I was proud of where my life had brought me.

Charlie smiled gently. "You'll be meeting my uncle today. I hope you're prepared."

"Otto Hillion?"

"More like Otto the Hellion, but yes," Charlie said with a smirk. "I love him dearly, but he's as ornery as they come."

"I love a challenge."

"Well, he'll give you that. He's not a mean man, but he has absolutely zero filter and cantankerous might as well be his middle name. I apologize now for anything shocking that may come from his mouth." Charlie sipped his coffee and sighed.

I immediately wanted to hear that satisfied sigh for the rest of my life.

I wanted to be the one making him sigh.

"Good?" I asked, saying a silent prayer my dick would behave. A hard-on in scrub pants was *not* appropriate coffee shop behavior.

Charlie blushed. "Sorry." He cleared his throat. "The first few times I came here, I got regular black coffee because I was embarrassed to order something that seemed...I don't know...frou-frou? But I finally challenged myself to order it the way I really wanted it and it's quickly becoming one of the best parts of my day." His eyes went wide and he cleared his throat. "And I have absolutely zero idea why I just told you that. I'm sorry, I don't usually run my mouth so much."

"No worries," I gave him a wink. "I like hearing you talk. And I love that we drink the best coffee order around. We're both new in town, so it's good to have a connection."

"A connection?" Charlie frowned.

"Yeah, if we're going to be friends, we need to have some sort of a connection. We actually have several. We're new in town, we like awesome coffee, and our love for Otto." *Please* I thought. Please let this guy want to be friends. And if there's a God above, please let him be interested in something more —more than friendship, more than a hookup. *More.*

"How do you know you're going to love Otto?" Charlie asked, his cheeks pink.

"I'm already looking forward to meeting him just from your description, I know he's going to be a favorite."

"We have another connection," Charlie said, his voice barely above a whisper.

"Yeah? What's that? Devilishly handsome? Fantastically gay? Amazing people?"

Charlie's eyes went wide and he sputtered. "Oh, um, I don't know about any of that. I just meant we're neighbors."

I cocked my head and tried to picture the two houses next to my new place. "Are you sure?"

"Well, backyard neighbors. I'm pretty sure Jo Ellen mentioned you're moving in behind where Otto and I just moved."

Recognition dawned. "You're in Harley's old place? With the guest cottage? I looked at that one, *loved* the cottage, but it seemed a waste for one person to have two homes." I winked. "Well, this is perfect. Backdoor friends are best."

Charlie's cheeks pinked and he bit his lip.

I thought over what I'd said. *Backdoor friends are best.* Surely, he wasn't taking that in a sexually suggestive way, right? I raised my brow.

Charlie ran a hand over his face. "Sorry, just something Otto said the other day. The man is a menace."

I chuckled and did *not* allow myself to think about any type of backdoor activities with Charlie other than being friends and neighbors—at least not right in the middle of the coffee shop. "Makes me want to meet him more and more." I sipped my coffee and studied Charlie over the cup. He seemed nervous. Or maybe it wasn't so much nervous as uncomfortable. Almost like he was waiting on something bad to happen. "So, about those other connections," I hedged.

"I like to think I'm a good person," Charlie said, dipping his head.

"Well, I already know you're probably the most handsome man in Briarton." My cheeks flushed. I was seriously flirting with my new client's nephew. That probably wasn't a good idea, but I couldn't help it. Charlie was so easy to talk to and I'd felt something from the moment his fingers brushed mine. I wanted to know this man.

"Have you seen the owners of this shop?" Charlie countered.

"Morgan and Justin? Yeah, crazy hot." I nudged his knee under the table. "But they're happily married so they don't count." I sipped my coffee and winked. "This is when you could say I'm the most handsome man you've seen in town, too."

Charlie smirked. "We just skipping over the confirmation of fantastically gay?"

I raised a brow.

"Yeah, okay. You're definitely easy on the eyes." Charlie's cheeks flamed. "Oh my God, I can't believe you got me to say that." He studied his cup. "Did you tell Justin to put something in my coffee? I never talk like this."

I cocked my head. "Like what?"

He gestured between us. "Like this. Just easy back and forth. The last time I fell into such an easy conversation was with Stella."

"Who's Stella?" An abnormal surge of jealousy raced through me at the thought of someone else knowing Charlie in the way I hoped to know him. Which was absolutely crazy; I was experienced in quite a few random hookups and casual dating situations I'd sometimes hoped would become more, but I didn't think I'd ever met someone new and so immediately wanted to know him and be something more with him.

"My best friend. I'm a total introvert, but I was forcing myself to get to the gym. She struck up a conversation and we ended up living together for ten years." Charlie smiled fondly.

"She didn't come with you to Briarton?"

"Nah, she's traveling the world. She will always have a place here with me if she decides to come home, but I think she's likely to float around for a while. She's enjoying finding herself." He chuckled. "And sleeping with every willing woman she comes across in her travels."

"So, Stella and I are both extroverts. Like a good conversation, know a fabulous guy when we see one, have every intention of getting to know said fabulous guy..." I trailed off.

"You both must have magic because this is the longest conversation I've had with anyone outside of Stella or Otto in...well, probably my entire life." Charlie pursed his lips. "That sounds pathetic."

"Nah, you're just choosy." I sipped my coffee. "So, Charlie Hillion, what do you do?"

He stared at me, unblinking, for a moment before shaking his head and giving a tiny smile. "I'm a writer. So, I spend most of my days at home with my words and my cats."

My eyes went wide and a smile filled my face. "You have cats? No way. So do I. See? Another connection." I pulled out my phone and scrolled to my pictures. "The yellow and white one is CoJack and the yellow orange one is Cheddar."

"That's adorable. They're so cute. Creative names, maybe *you* should be the writer." Charlie grinned as he turned his phone toward me. "The black one is Cricket and the tiger one is Hopper."

"Oh my God, they're gorgeous. Okay, what's the story with the names? Mine are pretty smack-you-in-the-face obvious once you see them."

Charlie shrugged. "When they were kittens, they jumped and pounced constantly. Like more than any cats I'd ever seen. I took them to the vet because I was worried something was wrong with them; they'd move across the floor jumping. He assured me everything was fine and it was just their way of exploring. They eventually grew out of it, but the names stuck."

"Too cute. Kinda works with their coloring. Black for the cricket, the grayish color for a grasshopper." I sipped my drink, unwilling to finish it too soon and have no good excuse to continue our chat.

"My thoughts exactly. They're great cats." Charlie put his phone to the side. "How long have you been a nurse?"

"Well, I'm forty-five," I started but paused when Charlie's face lit up. "What?"

"Nothing," he said with a blush, "it's just there's another connection. I'm forty-five."

"Destiny," I whispered with a wink. "Anyway, I've been a nurse for over twenty years."

"Always doing the in-home stuff?"

I shook my head. "No, I started in the ER. That was exciting and definitely kept me on my toes, but I didn't make it long—too easy to burn out after seeing a lot of bad shit that's beyond your help. Then I moved to the oncology floor. That was a good fit for a while."

"Wow, that has to be a really difficult position."

I shrugged. "It *is*, but it was also good for me. Obviously, I'm a big guy, so my strength is always useful in patient moves and whatever. But I'm also pretty soft-spoken and a good listener, so the patients liked talking to me."

"Why'd you leave?"

Frowning and staring at my cup, I shook my head. "We had a lot of great success stories, but the losses just got to me too much. Especially the patients with young children or the younger patients themselves—it got too hard for me."

"Where'd you go after that?"

"I got out of the hospital setting and went to work in a top-notch general practitioner's office. I liked it, but it wasn't *the* perfect job for me. I used it as a nice little break. The work was easy, but I got twitchy after a while." I tapped my fingers on the table. "Moved to a practice specializing in geriatrics and absolutely loved it. After a bit, I decided to try my hand at the in-home stuff and I immediately fell in love. I've been doing it for five years now and I can't imagine doing anything else."

"How'd you end up in Briarton?" Charlie asked.

"I was enjoying my job in the city, but knew I was looking for a change of scenery. I grew up in a city and had basically spent my whole life in one city or another, I wanted a change of pace. I started perusing job openings and saw Dr. Pierce was looking for a nurse who would do home health care with certain patients. I applied, had my interview, he loved me—of course—and I moved here. Lived in the backroom at his office for a bit before the Werkly's house went up and I grabbed it."

"You still in touch with your parents?" Charlie asked.

I snorted. "Negative."

Charlie grimaced. "Sorry, that was too personal."

"No, not at all. My entire family is highly conservative. They're big names in the political world and expected me to do the same." I shook my head. "They pretended to be supportive when I came out, but they demanded I keep *that part of my life* discreet. I met their demands for a lot longer than I care to admit. They hated I was a nurse instead of a doctor and constantly harassed me about joining them in their political work." I finished off my coffee and pushed the cup to the side. "I'd never had much luck in dating—but that can be a different story for a different day—but there was a day when I was upset about one more guy saying goodbye and my parents called me to dinner at their house to start in on me again and I just lost it. I blew up; told them I'd spent too long hiding myself for them. I'd *never* join them, I'd never become a doctor, and I'd never not be gay. I moved three states away and I haven't spoken to them since."

"Wow, that's a lot. Sounds like you're better off without them." Charlie glanced at his watch. "Speaking of different stories for different days, *I* have stories to write and a deadline to meet. I've *got* to go, but maybe we'll see each other again and I can share my family story and you can tell me about your bad luck in dating?"

The look of hope on his face—mixed with a something close to dread—filled my heart and had me fighting back the urge to give a fist pump.

"For sure. Are you going to be there when I meet Otto today?"

He nodded. "I can be, if it's best for you."

"It would help for you to hear all of what I'll be doing and whatnot. Maybe come for the second bit after I've had a chance to get to know him?"

"Perfect."

"And we *are* neighbors now. It's not like we can't chat over the fence or even walk over and share a beer by the fire pit," I said with a wink. "I definitely would like to get to know you more." At the look of terror mixed with amazement in his eyes, I went on. "Friends first. I need a friend in town." I grinned. "But I'm not opposed to something more if it ever comes to that."

Charlie sputtered, but the blush and smile that filled his face were too hard to ignore. "Um, yeah. Sounds good. I'll, um, see you at Otto's later." He rushed to stand up, bumping the table and nearly toppling his chair as he all but ran from the coffee shop.

I couldn't help the hopeful fluttering in my chest.

Charlie Hillion was different than any man I'd ever met and I wanted to know him inside and out.

"That went well," Justin said as he beamed at me from

the next table. He finished wiping the surface and indicated to a couple they could have the spot.

"It did, indeed," I agreed. "Do you know him well?"

"Not really. At first, he seemed really aloof and standoffish, but the more he's been around and kinda settled in with folks the more I can see he just takes a while to get to know people. He seems pretty reserved." Justin wiped down another table. "Completely unlike his uncle. That man is a hoot."

"So I've heard."

"My advice with Charlie—not that you asked, but I'm a giver like that—is to go the friend route first. He doesn't seem like the type of guy who just falls into something hot and heavy." Justin shrugged. "At least not from my interactions with him. He seems to need some time to warm up to people."

I thought about Charlie's smiles and how it had felt like we were bonding over our little connections. My thoughts must have shown on my face because Justin smirked.

"Yeah, yeah, I'd agree he seemed pretty at-ease with you, but I still wouldn't rush anything."

Standing, I hefted my bag to my shoulder. "I wouldn't say he was *at-ease* so much as he was at least willing to let his guard down a bit." I frowned. "Why does everyone assume I'm going to just jump into bed?" I asked in a curious whisper after checking to be sure no one was within earshot. "Every damn guy in my past was more concerned about getting me to fuck him than getting to know me. I'm not that type of guy."

"Whoa." Justin held up his hands. "I wasn't assuming anything. I don't know the first thing about your types or usual dating situations."

I snorted. "Dating situations aren't really something I have a lot of experience with."

"Still, I'm not saying you're the type to just want something quick, one and done. My point was just you and Charlie seemed to be hitting it off, but I wouldn't rush things with him unless he gives off vibes that's what he's wanting."

"Yeah," I sighed. "I get it. Sorry for getting snappy."

It was Justin's turn to snort. "You're the least snappy person I've ever met. You're like this big ol' soft-spoken teddy bear."

We'd made our way toward the door and I was glad the lunch rush had slowed so I had the time to chat with Justin. "I love me, but it gets so tiring to constantly be stereotyped. What you know to be a soft-spoken teddy bear because you've taken the time to know me beyond my physical appearance, other guys see as just a big, burly guy they want to get under in bed."

"Their loss. Charlie doesn't seem to be that type of guy. I know nothing about his past, but I'm going to venture a guess he's not...you know what, no. It's not my place to even make guesses." Justin turned his head when Morgan called from the counter. "You and Charlie are both new to town. Make the most of it and you'll at least end up with a new friend. Maybe more. I'll be cheering you two on."

I smiled. "Thanks. Oh, I almost forgot. Ms. Lydia gave me money to get her some of your loose-leaf tea."

Justin gestured toward the counter and I followed him. Once I had Lydia's tea, I said a quick goodbye to Morgan and Justin and headed to my next appointment.

THREE
CHARLIE

I COULDN'T WRITE to save my damn soul. Cricket and Hopper stared at me as if I'd lost my damned mind.

Ever since I was old enough to hold a pencil, I wrote when I was stressed or happy or sad. Writing was a way for me to escape my feelings and immerse myself in a different world away from whatever was bothering me. Most of the writing I did when I was stressed or upset never saw the light of day outside of my journal of random thoughts. Some of the writing I did when I needed to escape ended up being some of the best parts of my published work.

But even an hour after meeting Nixon Riley, I hadn't been able to calm the fuck down enough to write a single word.

Which both excited and terrified me.

I'd never met anyone—not even Stella had had such a rock-me-to-my-core effect on me—who'd made me feel like Nix had. From the moment our hands brushed as we reached for the coffee cup, there'd been some sort of searing awareness traveling through my body.

Nix was different.

Nix was gorgeous.

Nix wanted to get to know me.

And I wanted to get to know him. He wasn't the first guy I'd ever hoped to get to know better, but he was definitely the first guy who had ever thrown me for such a loop I couldn't even gather myself enough to put words on paper.

I'd never met someone and so immediately felt a connection with them. And it wasn't all the superficial connections—although, those were helpful and it was super cute how Nix kept pointing them out—it was the actual emotional connection I felt to him. Like he'd thrown out a tether and kept gently pulling me toward him.

Don't get me wrong, there was no way—even if it was offered, which I was pretty darn sure it wasn't going to be—I could just fall into bed with Nix. Yes, there were immediate connections, both actual and emotional, between us—at least, there were emotional pulls on my end—but it wasn't like I *knew* him. I was still demisexual and sex for the sake of sex with someone I didn't know well still wasn't my thing.

I paced my office, my heart beating a million miles a minute, my arms tucked behind my head.

But Nix made me feel as if he *wanted* to sit and chat with me. Like he truly did want to grab a beer and sit on the patio with me.

No other guy had ever made me feel that way. They were all usually put off by my standoffishness and didn't give me a chance to get to know them.

You weren't that way with Nix.

I frowned. That was the truth. It had been the weirdest feeling to have a complete stranger invite me to sit down and I didn't want to immediately bolt. Well, I wanted to, but the feeling wasn't as strong as usual.

And how in the hell had Nix got me chatting so easily? Talking to him seemed as easy as breathing.

Maybe he's your person.

Oh God.

My gut clenched.

My entire adult life—especially after coming out and figuring out I was demi—one of my only hopes was I'd find that person. The one who loved me for me, the missing piece to my puzzle.

There was *no way* I could let myself even contemplate that a man I met for the first time and talked to for less than an hour could possibly be *my person*.

Right?

I shook my head and continued to pace.

But it would make sense in a way because no one else had ever had such a pull on me. Yeah, Stella had reeled me in but we had a completely platonic relationship. Nix had lassoed me completely and—while I wasn't ready to burn up the sheets with him; thinking about sex was one thing, actually doing it was something else entirely—I wasn't averse to thinking about what we could maybe become to one another after a bit of time.

Did that make him my person?

Oh God, could I claim him as my person if he didn't feel the same way?

What if he found out how inexperienced I was?

What if he gave some effort to get to know me and found me completely and utterly lacking?

What if all he wanted was sex with no strings?

My stomach rolled with a wave of nausea as I thought of the heart-fluttering experience I'd had with Nix and how badly I wanted something more to come from it. Even if just friendship.

If he didn't want that, I wasn't sure my heart and psyche could withstand the disappointment.

I checked my watch. I had exactly two hours until I needed to head to Otto's to meet with him and Nix.

I grabbed a journal and sat down, determined to get the thoughts and feelings out of my head so I could turn my attention to my work-in-progress. Deadlines didn't wait for a forty-five-year old man realizing he had a crush.

When I emerged from my house two hours later, I felt slightly better. I'd done twenty minutes of free writing and tried to clear my head. My work in progress was now two thousand words longer. And I was about to crawl out of my skin with excitement over seeing Nix again.

The feeling was so damn foreign to me.

I looked forward to seeing Otto. I looked forward to spending time with Stella.

I'd *never* known another guy long enough to be looking forward to seeing him.

In the past, there'd been men I'd met and I'd gotten a tiny inkling I'd *maybe* want to get to know them or see them more. But they'd give up on me before it even got to that point. Maybe I'd only met really shallow men. Or maybe some of them were like me and they thought *I* wasn't willing to get to know them.

Or maybe you were just destined to end up in Briarton and meet the man of your dreams.

I cleared my throat and smiled to myself as I approached Otto's door. Turned out my imagination was a romantic and believed in fate. A shiver traveled through me. Honestly, I wasn't against the notion. But I was getting *way* too far ahead of myself.

Nix made it seem like he'd be more than willing to hang out, get to know you, be friends and possibly more.

My heart plummeted. Thinking about Nix and the type of guys he probably liked, I doubted I had much of a chance in the *more* department once he realized I was pretty much a damn forty-five-year-old loser virgin.

Stop. You have very valid reasons for being as inexperienced as you are. And even if you didn't have reasons, it's nobody's place to judge you for it. Whether by choice or circumstance or a combo of both, you have every right to come into your sexual exploration and experiences later in life.

I took a deep breath and closed my eyes before opening Otto's door. It was an argument I had with myself and Stella quite often. I knew my head and my best friend were right, but that didn't make it any easier for an introverted, demisexual, gay man with social anxieties to accept just one more thing that made me different.

Nix and I could get to know each other and see where things went from there.

A fluttery sensation tickled deep in my belly as I realized Nix was the first person outside of my uncle and best friend who I already felt as if I knew as more than a passing acquaintance or awkward attempted relationship.

As I opened the door, I heard Otto's voice.

"Probably should knock next time," Otto said to me with a mischievous grin. "We just finished the anal exam and things got a little steamy."

"Oh my God," I groaned.

Nix laughed out loud. "We did nothing of the sort, old man. Be careful or I'll give you enough anti-diarrhea medication to bind you up for a week."

Otto pressed a hand to his chest. "You wouldn't. Do you know how important bowel movements are to the elderly? Aside from a little oral action or a clandestine rendezvous with my dildo, a satisfying poop is sometimes the highlight of my day—hell, sometimes of my week. Don't threaten to take that from me."

Nix laughed, completely unphased by Otto's diatribe on bowel movements. "Then don't insinuate we were doing anything other than behaving as medical professional and well-behaved patient." He leaned in and pretended to whisper to my uncle. "I'm launching a campaign to convince this one here to accept the very open position of being my friend. Level one, friendship. Level two, my goal is to ask for a date. Level three, if all is going well, I may throw caution to the wind and ask for a kiss." Nix gave me a wink as my heart nearly galloped out of my chest and I glanced around for a place to sit down before my knees gave out.

Otto looked between Nix and me and smiled broadly. "Well, I see introductions aren't needed." To Nix he said, "I like the campaign premise. Do you need supporters? I can throw money at your cause. If you promise to keep me on a regular bathroom schedule, I'll offer up tips and secrets to help with your goals."

I crossed my arms over my chest and attempted to look annoyed, but I couldn't do it. Nix—this gorgeous, soft-spoken beefcake with the prettiest blond hair, blue eyes, and scruffy chin; this man who looked as if he could pick me up with one hand and break me in two without breaking a sweat. He'd thought about me to the point where he had a plan to get to know me and ask for a date and a kiss?

Had I died and gone to Heaven?

"I'm in the room," I deadpanned, but couldn't help the tiny smile teasing my lips when Nix grinned at me. "No telling stories on me or I'll hide your sex toys and deactivate your porn subscription." I wagged my finger at my uncle.

Otto narrowed his eyes. "Fine. But I'm not going to sit by and let either of you boys fuck something up. If I see there's an issue needing addressed and you two can't pull your heads from your asses, I'm going to speak up." He turned to Nix. "What are your thoughts on getting me some Viagra?"

Nix rolled his eyes and laughed. "You already have a prescription. Do you feel like you need a refill?"

"I need more than a couple pills a month. I can't keep up

with my sexual appetite with only a couple a month," Otto griped.

"I'll get you updated to five a month," Nix said. "If you find you're entertaining enough sexual partners to need more than that on a consistent basis, we can talk." He pointed his finger at Otto. "But if you're having sex that much, first, congrats and I'm jealous."

I coughed and nearly choked on my attempt to hide my laughter. "That's what I said," I whispered to Nix and my uncle beamed.

"Second, we need to make sure we're talking about safe sex practices," Nix advised.

"I got negative test results last time I was in at Dr. Pierce's," Otto argued.

"Yeah, well, not everyone is as lucky. Seniors are at high risk. Chlamydia increased in people sixty-five and older by thirty-one percent in a four-year-period. Syphilis among the same age group increased by fifty-two percent," Nix rattled off statistics. "With the availability of Viagra for men and hormone replacement therapies for post-menopausal women, sex in seniors is happening more and more. The spread of sexually transmitted infections in nursing homes is rampant." Nix scribbled something in his notebook. "I'm glad Dr. Pierce ran tests—a lot of doctors don't think about elderly patients being at risk—but you do need to be careful. Pregnancy may not be a worry, but an STI can wreak havoc on a more fragile immune system. It can also mess with medication effectiveness." Nix closed his notebook. "If you think being constipated ruins your day, just wait until you're dealing with painful urination, penis discharge, and pissing blood."

Otto's face was priceless. "Damn man, major boner killer."

Nix shrugged. "I'm just saying. Wear a condom. Men are a

hot commodity in the senior community—both women and men are looking for attractive and available sexual partners and most will do whatever it takes to keep them—you need to make sure you're protecting yourself."

"Maybe I'll just stick to self-satisfying myself for a while. It's quicker, easier, and I always get off—who knows what you like better than yourself?" Otto yawned.

"I'm going to scan these notes and send them to Charlie and Dr. Pierce," Nix said. "I'm scheduled to pop in Monday, Wednesday, Friday, and Sunday so I hope you're ready for that." Nix gave my uncle a charming grin. "We already talked about what I'd do when I'm here, but I'm going to fill in Charlie. We'll take our conversation outside so you can grab a nap."

Otto shuffled to the couch and settled in with a blanket. "We're neighbors. I already feel like we're friends. Don't be a stranger in the evenings and unscheduled days. We'll be here. I miss chatting on the patio with a beer." He pointed a finger at me. "Yeah, I know, no beer. But that makes the chatting with friends all the more important."

I stood by awkwardly as my uncle's eyes fluttered closed and Nix took care of his responsibilities.

"Is this charliehillion6976 email still a good one to send the notes to?" Nix asked with a gleam in his eyes.

My cheeks heated and I nodded. "Yeah, I've got a folder ready for whatever you send."

"What's the number for?" Nix asked as he worked.

"My birthday. June 9, 1976."

Nix gave a nod. "Ah, a Cancer."

"What about you?"

"May 5, 1976." Nix packed away his portable scanner and organized his bag.

"A Cinco de Mayo baby. Do you celebrate your birthday with tacos and margaritas?" I asked, suddenly sad we'd missed Nix's birthday because it would have been a built-in reason to ask him to come to dinner.

"That I do," Nix answered. "But I like tacos and margaritas *anytime*."

"Same."

"You wanna come see my new place? Maybe we could make tacos and margs for dinner and have Otto come over? My evening is free if you'd like to hang out." Nix's cheeks blushed a delicious shade of pink and that tether between us tugged at my chest. How could I say no to his adorable request? But my anxiety ramped up.

"You want to hang out with me?"

Nix gave a frowny smile. "Why wouldn't I?"

"I'm not used to having many friends. Can't say very many people have ever wanted to devote the time to hanging out with me," I said with a shrug.

"Well, I'm not like other people." Nix hefted his bag onto his shoulder. "We're both new here, it makes complete sense we'd become friends. You're easy to talk to, I love your uncle, and tacos sound perfect for dinner. I think we're almost required to have dinner and hang out with all the connections we've discovered today."

Hardly able to believe my luck, I did my best to tamp down the grin struggling to take over my whole face. "Sounds fun."

FOUR

NIX

I HATED the sadness that passed over Charlie's beautiful face when he talked about not having many friends. I knew he had Stella and Otto—and I also knew a person didn't *need* hundreds of friends—but I could tell from the pain in his words he'd been hurt in the past when it came to the lack of friends.

Why in the world wouldn't people want to get to know Charlie? He was gorgeous and I loved the subtle ways he reacted to me. The blushes and grins, almost as if he was out of practice with how to interact with a man.

Otto had been pretty cryptic as he talked about his nephew. *"Just give him time. Charlie is a great guy, but he needs time to get to know people. He's a bit odd, doesn't love a lot of socializing, but once you're in, he's a friend for life. Too bad not many have ever given him that chance,"* Otto had said. *"And that applies ten-fold to his dating life and all that might entail."* He'd wagged a finger in my direction. *"He needs time but he also might need you to make the first move. And I've said more than I should. Just be patient and let him know you're willing to take your time."*

I thought back on those words. Maybe I was reading way

too much into what Otto had said, but I got the feeling maybe Charlie was as inexperienced in dating and sex as he was in the friendship department. For a fleeting second, that thought filled me with fear. Who the hell was I to introduce someone to dating and sex? It wasn't like I'd had much success in that department.

But then I thought of Charlie's sweet smiles and his disbelief I'd want to hang out with him and I realized maybe we were perfect for each other—like we were *meant* to meet.

Charlie didn't have a lot of experience and took a long time to get to know someone. I had experience but no one ever wanted to take the time to really *know* me beyond a quick fuck. I decided right then and there Charlie and I just *had* to be friends and if things moved beyond that, I'd be sure to make it perfect for him.

"Let's make a list of ingredients and hit the grocery. I can give you the grand tour after that," I suggested.

"That works." Charlie motioned for me to come to his place. "Let's check and see what I have on hand first."

When we walked through the backdoor, Charlie gave me an uncertain look. "You wanna see the place?"

I'd seen it empty when I was looking for a house, but I wasn't going to turn down seeing it again. The house was a cottage style with a lot of great updates and Charlie had made it feel warm and inviting.

He showed me around the downstairs as Cricket and Hopper followed us. The upstairs was home to Charlie's room and office. I loved how he'd filled the place with his belongings and I immediately felt at ease—like I was surrounded by Charlie and everything was *right*.

We ended up back down in the kitchen where he grabbed a pen and notepad while I played with the cats.

"I know I have a package of frozen beef," he said as he tapped the pen against his mouth.

"And I just bought some chicken, so we've got the meat covered." I smiled as the cats purred and rolled to their backs for belly rubs. After a bit, I stood and moved to the counter.

Taking a chance, I stepped close enough to read over his shoulder while he wrote *tomatoes*, *lettuce*, *avocado*, and *cilantro* on the list. "Is this okay?" I asked softly.

Charlie's breath caught in his throat, but he nodded. "You okay with cilantro? I know some people don't like it."

"Love it. Not a huge fan of onions or peppers though."

"Same." Charlie gave me a tiny grin. "Sour cream?"

"I've got that."

"Salsa?"

"Let's get some at Wayne's. I saw a fresh corn salsa there the other day that looked delicious. Is it weird I like salsa even though I don't love big chunks of onion?"

Charlie shook his head. "I like the juice part best. Maybe we should make our own. I like to use the food processor on the parts I don't love—it's mostly the crunch of the onions— and then we can mix up what we like."

"Perfect. Tomatoes, onions, cilantro, avocado, corn, that all sounds super good."

Charlie nodded and finished his list. "Oh, what about tortillas? Or shells?"

"I like soft tacos best."

"Me too. Let's get chips though." Charlie pulled out his phone. "I'm going to text Otto so he knows where I am. What time should I tell him to plan on dinner?"

"Let's plan on six." I waited for Charlie to grab his frozen beef and then we headed out after quick goodbyes to the cats.

We walked through the backyard to my house. Not gonna lie, I got a strange buzz thinking that our places were so close. Could it possibly get awkward if things didn't work out between us? Sure. But things were already so easy with

Charlie, I had a good feeling we'd have a friendship at minimum.

Upon walking through my backdoor, Charlie immediately placed the frozen beef on the counter and dropped to his knees to say hello to CoJack and Cheddar when they came scampering around the corner as we walked through the door. "You're beautiful, yes you are," he cooed.

When he stood up, he dipped his head. "Sorry, I'm a sucker for cats. My boys will be jealous I met new friends. What can I do to help?"

"No worries. We should get them together and let them play," I said. If the cats loved each other, would that give us more of a reason to see each other as often as possible? "Put the meat on a plate—they're in that cabinet. We can let it thaw while we're gone. Look in the fridge—you like that beer?"

Charlie gawked at me as if he wasn't sure what language I was speaking.

I smiled softly. He wasn't used to being in other people's homes. I pointed toward the cabinet. "Grab a plate, please."

He blinked his eyes and reached for a plate.

I took it from him and he opened the beef, placing it on the plate.

I then opened the refrigerator and pointed toward the beer. "You like this kind?"

Charlie tentatively peered over my shoulder. "Yeah, it's good."

"Okay, I have the alcohol and ice for margaritas. Can you put salt and lime on the list?" I pulled the chicken from the freezer and placed it on a separate plate to thaw. "You ready?"

Charlie glanced around and grabbed a pen from the counter. I loved he was already comfortable enough to do that—it was a small thing, but I was taking it as a victory.

Charlie gave a nod as he added salt and lime to the list. "Yep, let's go. Wayne's will have everything we need."

"You wanna drive or walk?"

"I'd rather walk if it's okay with you. I have to be sure I get enough movement each day—my job doesn't lend itself to a lot of moving around." Charlie folded the list neatly and slipped it in his pocket.

"Perfect. I love the fact we can walk almost anywhere in this town. The city was great and I didn't even bother with a vehicle, but I love this place because it's easy to walk *and* it's not teeming with people."

We headed down the sidewalk toward Wayne's Grocery.

"I love this little place," Charlie whispered as we entered the shop. He grabbed a cart and we started down the aisles.

I had a brief pang of longing as I thought of how we could do this—as a couple—if things worked out between us. Of course, I was getting ahead of myself because there was every chance we'd hit it off as friends and nothing more. From the little I knew, Charlie wasn't one to just hop right into bed with someone. And I was most definitely exhausted by my past of being expected to top anyone and everyone who bent over for me and then just stand by as they said goodbye after they got what they wanted.

But I wanted trips to the grocery store with Charlie, tacos and beer on the patio, hanging out with no expectations.

"I've been in here a couple times. They seem to have everything and then some." I grabbed a package of tortillas.

"I like that they try to keep it all local. From what Jo Ellen said, if you need something they don't have, they'll get it for you." Charlie held up a bag of tortilla chips and waited for my nod before adding them to the cart. "I think it would be fun to have a little shop like this."

I cocked my head and smiled in hopes of encouraging him to elaborate.

Charlie blushed and shrugged. "I've always wanted to own a small business. I do in a way as a self-published author, but I mean a little place like this seems like it would be rewarding and fun." He chuckled. "I know it's weird to hear that from a guy who barely leaves his house and almost has a nervous breakdown when asked to dinner by his handsome backdoor neighbor." Charlie bit his lip and shot a flirty look my way, making my heart beat fast because I figured his words and the look took a lot of bravery on his part. "But owning a business like this would force me to get out. In a town this small, I'd know people already or get to know them fairly quickly. I'd be helping people. I think something like this would be good for me." He leaned closer. "Don't let them hear me say it, but I already have things I'd do to improve on their greatness."

I laughed and wanted to step closer and kiss his cheek. "Better watch for a *For Sale* sign."

"From your lips to God's ears. But that's a stretch even for my writer imagination."

We approached the produce section.

"Never know. Speak it, claim it as yours, maybe the universe has a plan for you." I picked up two avocados and put them in the cart.

By the time we were done with our grocery shopping, I would have sworn Charlie and I had been friends since childhood. He was the easiest guy to talk to. I adored the fact we were just chatting about anything and everything with no tension and expectations about dates or sex.

We each carried two reusable grocery bags into my house and fell into an easy rhythm of unpacking.

"Want to see the place?" I asked, glad I'd waited because Charlie seemed more comfortable around me than he had before.

"Definitely. This place wasn't up for sale when we were looking."

"I think you may have missed it by a few days. Probably not as great a set-up as you have for Otto. But I really like it." I started the tour and showed Charlie all the rooms and bathrooms.

My house was a bungalow style and I'd brought most of my furniture from my place in the city. I kept everything pretty contemporary and comfortable. Somehow, just having Charlie in my space made it feel more like a home and that struck me as both heartwarming and crazy.

"Great place. I love it." Charlie rubbed his hands down his pants as we returned to the kitchen. "Should we start the food prep?"

"Yeah, let's get to work. Do you want a margarita while we prep?"

Charlie gave a quick nod. "I'll cut up the limes."

"You want regular or strawberry? I have strawberry simple syrup."

His eyes lit up at the mention of strawberry. "Definitely strawberry. I'm always down for anything sweet."

We set to work making the margaritas.

"Have you always been a writer?" I asked as I poured the slushy mixture into the two glasses Charlie had rimmed in a mixture of sugar and margarita salt.

"In some form or another," he answered before taking a sip and humming his appreciation. "I wrote for the school paper in high school. Eventually became the editor. Wrote for the newspaper in college. I took a lot of writing classes and really got into fiction writing in college. I've had some sort of job involving writing for my entire career. Lucked out and got accepted by a publisher after I started ghost writing and now I'm enjoying the self-publishing aspect as well."

"I admire your ability to work for yourself," I said and took a drink. "Damn, that's good."

"The self-publishing is definitely the hardest for me because I don't have a publisher breathing down my neck about deadlines." Charlie took another drink before gathering vegetables on the counter. "I'm not sure I'd be as disciplined and successful with self-publishing if I hadn't already had years of learning how to meet deadlines and put my ass in the chair and write."

I pulled out the food processor. "I'm putting you in charge of the salsa. I'll cook the corn and cut it off the cob."

We fell into an easy rhythm of working and talking.

"So, you know about my parents," I hedged.

Charlie wrinkled his nose. "I swear to God, you must exude truth serum or something. My voice is going to be hoarse from all the talking I've been doing. It's like you flipped a switch on me and I can't stop the verbal spillage."

I winced. "Sorry, if it's too much, you don't have to tell me."

He shook his head, the look on his face one that showed me he was in awe of the fact he was so willing to talk. "No, it's not that. I just don't usually talk this much. I'm never really comfortable talking about myself. You just make it easy."

"I'm honored." I lifted my glass and held it out toward him. "To friends who are always comfortable enough to talk and share with each other."

Charlie's eyes sparkled as his cheeks pinked and he picked up his own glass and clanked it with mine. "I like that." He took a drink. "Margaritas at your place may be my new favorite thing."

"Let's make it our thing," I answered with a wink, my stomach fluttering when Charlie blushed even pinker. I absolutely loved watching Charlie react to me.

"So, my dad..." Charlie started. "Well, let's just say Otto has always been more of a father to me than my actual dad."

"I take it he and his brother weren't a lot alike?"

Charlie shook his head. "It's weird—and kinda a gut punch—because Dad, his name was Orson, accepted Otto and his differences for the most part. Dad even accepted my mom's quirks and oddities. But for some reason, he wasn't able to accept me. He told me often what a disappointment I was and how he'd never understand why I chose to be a... well, a word I won't use....and why couldn't I just be a normal kid." He sipped his drink, lost in thought. "It was really hard being a kid who already knew I was different, who lost my mom at such a young age I barely remembered her, and had to try to navigate through a world where it was okay for my mom and uncle to be different, but my own differences were something my dad just wouldn't accept."

After walking around the counter, I stood close to Charlie. "Early friendship disclaimer, I'm a hugger. If you're not comfortable with it, we can fist bump."

Charlie's eyes went wide.

"Can I give you a hug?" I asked. He nodded slightly and I wrapped him in my arms. "I'm so very sorry you had to deal with having a parent like that."

A shudder traveled through Charlie and he all but melted into my body. His reaction made me wonder how empty his bucket was when it came to physical affection.

With a sigh, almost as if he didn't want to, Charlie pulled away. "Sorry, I don't get a lot of opportunities for hugs and I'm not one to want hugs from strangers."

"Good thing we're no longer strangers," I said with a pat to his back.

Charlie paused and gave a little smile. "We aren't, are we?"

I shook my head. "Doesn't feel like it."

"Do you always make friends this quickly?" he frowned.

"No. I had a lot of acquaintances and a few good friends in the different places I lived and worked, but I can honestly say I've never hit it off with someone like I have with you." It wasn't a lie or a line; Charlie was the easiest person in the world to talk to. Made me wonder just what kind of jerks he'd run into in his past who wouldn't give the time or effort to get to know him.

"Same. Well, not that I have a lot of acquaintances—but I'd consider Otto and Stella my two good friends. But I've never met someone I've so immediately felt comfortable talking to." Charlie bit his lip as if he maybe wanted to say more, but a knock sounded at the backdoor and I moved to let Otto in.

We spent the evening eating, drinking, laughing, chatting, and playing with CoJack and Cheddar—my babies were in hog heaven with all the attention. When Otto announced he wanted to get home to watch the early news before heading to bed, I fought back a protest.

Charlie eyed me for a moment before swallowing. "How about I get Otto home and come back to help clean up?"

It wasn't as if I *needed* help cleaning up, but I wasn't going to turn down more time with Charlie. "Sounds good."

Ten minutes later, Charlie and I were at the kitchen sink washing and drying dishes.

"You want that beer by the fire before we call it a night?" I asked.

Charlie smiled. "Sure thing, we never did make it to beer, did we? The margaritas were too good."

We settled on my patio and I started a fire in the pit; conversation was easy and random, but it was good. Like we were sharing and tucking away tidbits about each other like squirrels gathering up acorns.

"This would be a good spot for a hot tub," Charlie mused.

"Exactly what I was thinking. Maybe I'll put one in next year." I liked the thought of *next year* and where things with Charlie and me might be by then.

"How many patients do you see a day?" Charlie asked.

"Usually two to four. I can fit in five if they aren't ones who need a lot of care. Three or four is the best set-up for me. A day with only two leaves me feeling unproductive."

"I bet you have some good stories; elderly people can be funny."

"You have no idea. I'm guessing Otto will give me plenty of stories to tell," I teased.

"No doubt about that." Charlie drank the rest of his beer and stood. "As great as this day has been, I've got words to write tomorrow, deadlines to meet. I need to get home and get some sleep."

A pang of disappointment shot through me and I stood to take Charlie's beer bottle. "Can we make this a regular thing?" I asked, probably sounding way too desperate.

Charlie stared at me for a moment before nodding. "As long as you let me host from time-to-time. My deck is nice."

I grinned. "For sure." I stepped closer and took Charlie's hand. "Listen, I definitely want to work on this friendship, but I need you to know I'm not against something more than friends. I don't want to push or rush, just wanted to put it out there."

Charlie's face lit up, but his expression fell just as quickly. "I'm demisexual," he said in a rush.

I nodded. "Okay. What does that mean for you?" The term was one I'd heard, but not one I had experience with.

He gawked as if he couldn't believe I was still standing there. "Um, it means I have no desire to have a sexual relationship with someone until I know them and feel a connection with them. It's not a cut and dry identity, but that's what it means for me." He ducked his head. "Since getting to know people has always been a struggle for me, it also means I'm *very* inexperienced—which I know sounds so lame at forty-five..."

I cupped his chin. "Hey, no. None of that. I think a lot of LGBTQ+ individuals come into their sexual experiences much later. There's nothing wrong with that." I caressed his cheek with my thumb. "Are you interested in a romantic relationship?"

Charlie nodded. "Very much so."

"Sexual?"

Another nod. "Definitely. But I've never felt comfortable enough with anyone to explore that. Don't get me wrong, I *want* sex. I just can't fathom having sex with someone I don't know, someone I'm not comfortable with."

I nodded and smiled. "Believe me, I get it. I'm not demisexual, but I totally get the desire to feel a connection with a person I'm going to bed with. Since you told me a bit about you, let me tell you a bit about me." I cleared my throat. "Sex started early for me, but it was never fulfilling. I was always expected to top—don't get me wrong, I like to top, but I'm vers so bottoming is great too—because men would see me and assume since I was this big, burly guy I only wanted one thing. I've always felt very used in sexual situations. Like the men seem interested and whatever just until they get me to fuck them and then they split."

"So, what are you looking for?" Charlie whispered.

"I'm looking for an actual relationship. Someone I connect with, someone I enjoy spending time with, someone who wants me for more than just sex." My heart clawed its way into my throat as I spoke. *Please don't let this scare him away.*

Charlie reached up and took my hand, holding it gently against his cheek. "That sounds amazing."

"You want the same?"

He nodded.

"I don't know the boundaries here," I hedged.

"Ask. I'll tell you if it's something I can't handle yet." Charlie pressed his cheek into our hands. "But I've got to be completely honest, *no one* has ever gotten me to talk so openly. No one has ever made me feel such a connection. Stella did those things, but neither of us had any sexual interest in the other." His cheeks pinked in the firelight as he realized he'd just spilled the beans on his sexual interest in me. "The thought of sex with you isn't something I could do tonight, but you're the first man I've ever known who I think I could probably eventually go to bed with. I trust you and I like you—I want to know you better." His eyes caught mine. "So, if there's something you want to ask, go for it. I'll be honest with you."

"I want another hug." I bit my lip. "And a kiss would be amazing if you're feeling it."

Charlie gasped, a soft sound that went straight to my cock, and nodded. "I've only kissed a few people and they were a very long time ago."

"Doesn't matter. Just means your first real kisses are mine and there's nothing I want more than that." I wrapped a loose arm around Charlie's waist and pulled him close. "Put your arms where they feel comfortable." I sighed into him when he wrapped his arms around my neck. With my other hand, I tipped up his chin and brushed a light kiss over his lips.

When Charlie whimpered, my knees nearly gave way.

"Charlie," I whispered against his mouth.

He moaned and leaned into the kiss, pressing our soft, warm lips together. When he opened his mouth just slightly, I fought the urge to explore his mouth with my tongue. Instead, I increased the pressure of my lips on his, savoring the flavor of his kiss and soaking up the whimpery moans coming from the man I knew without a doubt had, at that very moment, turned my world upside down.

Charlie broke the kiss and stepped away, his hands to his lips, his chest heaving. "Was that okay?"

I laughed and opened my arms. Charlie stepped into my embrace and I held him tightly against me. "That was so, *so* very much okay."

"I'm sorry I can't give you more right now," Charlie whispered into my neck.

"That was plenty. I'm not looking for just a fuck, Charlie. I want walks and grocery trips, beers by the fire, taco dinners, and dates." I tipped his chin and feathered a kiss over his lips. "And I want those things with you. It's crazy to me how badly I want all of that with someone I just met, but nobody in my life has ever made me feel what you've made me feel. Like everything in my past was just practice—showing me what I didn't want—and getting me prepared for when I met you."

"Like you've met your person?" Charlie whispered. "Sorry, that's probably dumb…"

My heart caught in my throat and I palmed his cheek. "Yeah, it's *exactly* like that."

He smiled and pressed his forehead against mine. "I know the feeling. It's something I've always wanted but never thought I'd get."

"We've got all the time in the world. You call the shots here, Charlie. Tell me what you want and when you want it." I gave him another quick kiss.

"Can you make some of the moves and let me opt in or out?"

"Absolutely. Now, as much as I hate for the night to end, we both have jobs to get to tomorrow. Is it okay if I get your number from Otto's information so I can text you?"

Charlie nodded. "Yeah. I put my phone on do not disturb while I'm writing, but I'll check it on breaks."

"Perfect." I wrapped my arms around him again and hugged him close. "Thank you for an amazing day. Sleep tight."

"You, too." He backed away and bit his lip. "We'll talk tomorrow?"

"Count on it."

I couldn't help the goofy grin that filled my face as I watched Charlie walk through the backyard to his house.

FIVE

CHARLIE

"OH MY GOD," Stella squealed on the other end of the phone a few weeks later, "that's it. I'm coming back so I can meet your person."

I chuckled nervously and ran a hand over my face as I paced my office and talked to my best friend. I'd spent the last few weeks pouring words into my stories—fueled by the energy of excited, hopeful anticipation and nearly crippling uncertainty about whatever was going on between me and Nix. I'd kept things to myself for as long as I could, but when Stella called, I'd gratefully put away my work for the day and spilled my guts to her.

As promised, Nix had texted me the day after we'd met and we'd settled into an easy back and forth chat every day between my writing sprints and his patients. Over the last few weeks I'd gathered courage and asked Nix to go for a walk, grab a coffee, or come over for dinner—if he didn't beat me to the punch and invite me to do those things first.

We'd been spending a lot of time together and the strong connection from day one had grown exponentially. We'd been doing a lot of soft touches, hand holding, and experimental kissing in addition to chatting as if we'd known each other for years. Every moment we spent together brought us closer and closer. I finally knew what it meant to have a connection with someone—in Nix, I'd found not only an emotional and romantic attraction, but a sexual one, too, and I was anxiously anticipating the next step in whatever this thing between us was.

"Is it stupid crazy to even consider he's my person? I mean, I just met the man." I ran a jittery hand through my hair. "I mean, we've known each other for a while now, but I was already feeling this way back when I first met him."

"Doll, I think this is one of those situations where when you know, you know. If you claimed every man you met was your person, if you went gaga over guys you just met, if you reacted this way with every man, I'd question the validity of what you're feeling for Nix," Stella explained. "But I've known you for over ten years and you've never once reacted this way toward anyone. Maybe he's your soul mate."

"Soul mate?" I repeated. I mulled over the word. The concept wasn't something I'd given much thought to, but the instant connection between Nix and me almost made me think *soul mates* was the right term. I chewed my thumbnail. "What if that's because no one else has taken the time to get to know me? What if I'm just feeling this way because Nix threw me a bone and I'm desperate?"

"Shut up," Stella said. "Look, part of the reason you've never made a connection with a man is because you never see a reason to go out and socialize. That right there decreases your chances. Add to it the guys you've happened to meet end up being some sort of mixture of introverts like you or interested only in sex or complete douchebags or just really bad at building a relationship, and you've got a spectacular mess of no way, no how when it comes to meeting people and getting to know them."

"That doesn't prove I'm not just reacting this way because Nix took time to get to know me."

"True." A door closed on Stella's side of the call and I could tell she'd walked into the little room she'd rented in Italy. "But you know yourself. You know even if a guy spent an entire day talking to you, you wouldn't get all fluttery about them if you didn't feel a connection, a pull."

"But I've never felt a connection, a pull," I argued. "How do I know this isn't just me excited that someone finally took time for me?"

Stella groaned. "I guess you don't know. But I will say, as your best friend, I've seen you after a lunch date, a coffee date, a dinner date—yes, they've been few and far between—but you've never once returned from those things in such an adorable tizz over a guy." She sighed. "I've always felt so lucky you and I hit it off. I've never once thought you only opened up to me and allowed me to be your friend just because I was the only person who talked to you. I've seen you shut down attempts at casual conversation from a variety of people over the years—your gut, your psyche, your *whatever* always seems to instinctively *know* who it wants to let in and who it doesn't."

I scoffed. "Well, my *whatever* kinda sucks because it has effectively limited me to two friends and an abysmal love life."

Stella chuckled. "Yeah, but Otto and me are the most amazing two friends. And maybe all of your past has been leading up to you meeting the right guy at the right time. Maybe you and Nix have both been wading through all the bad so you could totally appreciate the good. I don't know him, but I can hear in your voice he's struck something deep inside—and that makes him a keeper in my book. Anyone who can give you such an adorable, breathless anticipation and excitement *has* to be a good guy. Plus, he *took the time* to get to know what an amazing person you are. That's gotta count for something."

My cheeks hurt from smiling. "He really is great. And Otto seems to adore him. And the boys liked him."

"What's his sign?" Stella asked.

"Oh, um, I don't know." I thought back to our conversation about birthdays. "His birthday is May 5."

"Ahhh, a Taurus, that actually makes perfect sense."

"Why?" Stella was very into astrology. I could barely remember my own sign.

"Well, I'd need to look at his moon and rising signs, but a Taurus matches well with your Cancer. Nix probably needs commitment, trust, honesty, straight forward communication. All of which he'll get from you."

"So, a Taurus matches with a Cancer. Does a Cancer match with a Taurus?" I seriously never took much time to learn or consider the signs, but I always loved to hear Stella talk about them.

"Your Cancer matches well with a Taurus, yes. You need affection and you need to feel special. You need someone caring and smart. A Taurus can give you all of that." Stella sighed happily. "The signs have spoken. It is so."

I laughed. "I have to say Nix has already shown me just how much I'm missing out on in the affection department. And he makes me feel special. He's definitely caring and smart." I thought about what she'd said regarding what Nix's sign was looking for. "I can definitely give commitment—I'm not saying I can promise forever, but I'm not looking for a one-off. I'm trustworthy, honest, and straight forward. Nix makes it easy to be that way—he's so easy to talk to."

"That's because you two are each other's missing pieces. I'm sure he's great, and so are you, but you two hit it off so perfectly because it was meant to be."

"You sound so sure. How can you even know that? You've

never met him." I paced. "Maybe I'm just infatuated and elaborating on his greatness."

"Charlie, doll, I've waited over ten years to hear this kind of excitement in your voice over something other than a manuscript. You and Nix have a connection."

I frowned as I glanced out my office window at Nix's house. Both my bedroom and office faced his place and I was pretty sure his bedroom window was the one directly within my line of sight. "We like the same coffee, we like cats, we're the same age. Those are all superficial connections."

"True," Stella said patiently. "But take those away. Take away every surface-level connection and what do you have?"

My heart danced in my chest. "A connection I've never felt before. It's like I've known him my whole life."

"You know I'm not one to throw caution to the wind." The smile was evident in her voice—we both knew *she* threw caution to the wind on an hourly basis, hence the fact she was traveling the world rather than being by my side during my life-changing moment. "At least not when it comes to you. But this thing with Nix isn't setting off any warning bells with you. I'm not getting any red flags. Otto already thinks the world of him…"

I snorted. "True. But that may just be because Nix followed through on the promise to get him more Viagra and has the right supplies to keep him pooping on a regular basis."

Stella laughed and I smiled at the loud, raucous sound. "If you're looking for my blessing, you've got it. If you're wanting advice, I say take the chance. You've never felt about someone the way you feel about Nix—not even guys you really *wanted* things to work out with, I *never* heard what I hear in your voice right now. Hug him, kiss him, take walks, buy groceries, go on dates, eat tacos, watch movies. Let things happen when they feel right."

As her words washed over me—making me want all of what she described—I panicked. "Oh my God, Stell. I have no clue what I'm doing when it comes to sex."

"Nonsense. Sex is easy. Do what feels good. I know you've watched porn—disclaimer, I'm *not* saying porn is realistic—and I know you've touched yourself." She shuddered. "The day I found your lube and sex toys will forever be burned into my brain."

I groaned. "Oh my God, I have *one* sex toy and it was a travel-size bottle of lube. Believe me, *hearing* your vibrator behind a closed door from the living room is also burned into my brain. Even worse was hearing *you.*"

"My date left me high and dry, I had to do something." She giggled and I groaned. "Okay, we're even. But like I was saying, you know what you like. You know the whole flap A in slot B procedure. You and Nix can work together to learn what each other likes, have fun with it."

Swallowing down the excited nausea at the thought of sex with Nix—how could I want something so badly while being scared to death of it?—I glanced at my phone screen as a text came through. "I want to ask him to do something this evening. Is that too desperate? Too clingy? Too much?"

"You guys have been hanging out pretty regularly, right?"

"Yeah, maybe he needs a break from me?"

Stella made a noise and I could picture her shrugging and waving her hand. "Won't hurt to ask. Nix seems like the type of guy who appreciates a person just being upfront about things. If he's got plans or doesn't want to do anything, he'll tell you." Something rustled on Stella's side of the call and she gave a little squeak of excitement. "Oh! My date's here. She's so damn gorgeous. Doesn't speak a word of English but that's not the part of her tongue I'm the most interested in. The woman knows how to..."

"Got it, I got it," I interrupted. "Have fun with Ms. Italian tongue."

Stella laughed and I heard her open the door and greet her date. "Let me know how things go with Nix. I seriously do want to visit and meet him. I love you."

"Love you, too. You've always got a place here. Be safe and have fun."

"Always."

The phone went dead.

Opening my texts, I saw a message from Nix.

Nix: *Thoughts on dinner with friends tonight?*

My heart began scrambling to my throat. Dinner with Nix? I could handle that—I'd be a nervous wreck, but I could handle it—each time we got together over the last few weeks had gotten easier.

Dinner with Nix and Otto.

Sure. Dinner with *friends*? Well, first off, I didn't really have any friends. Second, that sounded like a big group and a big group sounded terrible.

Before I could work myself into a panic, my phone buzzed.

Nix: *I was thinking of asking Harley, Jo Ellen, Justin, and Morgan to come to dinner at my place. Are you and Otto available?*

I sighed. Okay, that group of people I could handle. Would they consider me a friend? They were all friendly, easy-going people and I'd been around them more than once. The thought of dinner with them didn't send me into a nervous tailspin. Plus, dinner with them would be a reason to see Nix and that was a definite positive.

Me: I'm free. I'll check with Otto. What time and what can I bring?

Nix: Let's do 6:00. I was thinking a baked potato bar. Is that lame?

Me: Sounds fun. What can I bring?

Nix: Can you do butter, sour cream, and shredded cheese?

Me: Yep. See you then.

Nix sent a little kissy face and my chest nearly exploded. What did that mean? He was grateful I was bringing potato toppings? He wanted to kiss me? He was looking forward to seeing me?

I groaned and fisted my hair before flopping down on the loveseat in my office. Cricket and Hopper lazily stretched from their perches on the window sill and came to cuddle on my lap.

"Boys, I'm a mess. I don't think I realized how stressful life outside my introvert cocoon is." The cats stared at me as if I was an idiot. "I know, I know. I've always *wanted* to find the right guy, but I think I'd convinced myself it wasn't going to happen. I'm not exactly young."

Forty-five isn't ancient, goofball I could almost hear Stella saying.

She was right. Hell, Otto was still out there having fun at eighty, surely, I could do it. My unique combination of—well, of just being *me*—had made it so easy to miss out on friendships of any kind and so hard to build a relationship even if I'd wanted to. Meeting Nix had turned all of that on its head and left me shell-shocked.

As overwhelming and scary as it was to suddenly find myself in a situation where I so easily clicked with a man I found attractive and wanted to explore *more* with, it was also something I'd been waiting for my entire life. No matter how nervous I was about the whole thing, I wasn't going to miss out on the chance.

Stella and Otto were right. Nix and I ending up in Briarton and meeting each other was something akin to fate and I wasn't going to question it.

I just prayed I didn't end up brokenhearted.

PART of me was glad everyone could make it to dinner, but a tiny piece of me kinda wished everyone but Charlie already had plans so it could be just the two of us.

But no, having a group setting would be good for us both.

We both needed to get to know people around town.

And Charlie needed the safety net of having friends so he had no built-in reasons to avoid socializing from time-to-time. Not that I thought he had to become a social butterfly like his uncle, I just wanted him to be comfortable with people around town. A little place like Briarton didn't allow for anonymity the way a big city did.

A knock sounded at my door as I thumped down the steps, my hair still damp from my shower after work. CoJack and Cheddar both perked up, looked at me, looked at each other, and I swore I saw them shrug as if to say, *Might as well go see who it is; maybe someone to entertain us.*

I chuckled as my babies scampered toward the door.

Unable to hide my happy smile when I saw Charlie through the window, I yanked open the door.

Charlie ducked his head. "Sorry, I'm early. I came straight

from the store. I can just drop this stuff and come back later."

"No way, come in," I reached for his hand and pulled him close, the reusable grocery bag bumping our legs. Scanning his face for any signs he was uncomfortable, I brushed my knuckles over his cheek. "Hi."

Charlie's eyes danced and he leaned into my touch. "Hi."

We'd been building our friendship a lot over the last few weeks and what had started as a crazy-strong connection had blossomed into something I'd never experienced before. Friendship, romance, physical and sexual attraction, it was all there and had me in a swirl of excited anticipation.

"Otto coming later?" As selfish as it sounded, I wasn't at all upset to have Charlie to myself for a while.

"Uh, no." Charlie grinned. "He has a date."

"Damn, he's like the Energizer Bunny. I can only hope I'll still be going so strong at that age."

Charlie chuckled. "Right? I'm hoping I am, too. Missed too much of the first half of my life." His cheeks colored and he dipped his head, saying hi to the boys as CoJack and Cheddar rubbed against our legs.

Hope soared through me at the thought that *maybe* Charlie and I could find something together and enjoy the rest of our lives with each other.

"Can I kiss you?" I whispered, my forehead pressed to Charlie's.

I'd never known someone who identified as demisexual, but I'd been reading up on it. I knew there was debate on whether or not demisexual fit under the asexual umbrella along with graysexual, or gray ace, but a lot of what I read indicated it did. I also knew, just like there was no specific set of hard and fast rules for what it meant to be gay or lesbian or bi or trans, there were no specifics on what it meant to be demisexual. It made sense that the label would be different for each different person. The main thing I'd been able to gather, based on what Charlie had told me and what I'd read, was demisexual people might be romantically attracted and/or physically attracted to a person, but they weren't *sexually* attracted to a person unless or until a strong emotional bond was formed.

All of that had me feeling like I'd won the lottery because Charlie and I had formed some sort of crazy bond the moment his hand touched mine in Piping Hot. Maybe I was reading more into the pull I felt between us, but I really didn't think so. I swore Charlie was just as floored by what flamed to life so quickly between us.

He nodded and licked his lips as he tipped his chin up slightly to meet my mouth. "I've not done a lot and I may be terrible at it, but I really want to try some other things. Maybe not right this second," he smiled against my lips, "but I've never actually wanted sex with anyone and these feelings are kinda making me feel crazy."

"Stay after people leave tonight. We can do whatever you're comfortable with," I murmured against his mouth before flicking my tongue out to tease his bottom lip. Our little touches and kisses the past few weeks had been multifunctional—they were something we both wanted, they gave Charlie time to adjust, and they proved to me that he wasn't just hanging out with me to get sex.

With a little groan, Charlie blindly placed the bag on the counter next to us and wrapped his arms around my neck. Heat raced through me as he tilted his head and opened his mouth, inviting me inside to savor and explore. Our kiss was new and exciting, but it also felt as safe and comfortable as if we'd been kissing each other our entire lives.

I shifted our positions so Charlie's back was against the counter and moved to press kisses along his jawline and neck when he moaned. I pushed against him and Charlie popped his ass up onto the counter, spreading his legs and deepening the kiss.

"I could kiss you all damn night," I growled, burying my face in his neck, loving the way he dropped his head back against the cabinet to allow me better access. The fact I had a gorgeous man in my arms without the unspoken understanding that all he wanted from me was a hard and fast fuck had my heart beating a million miles a minute.

"There's so much I want to do," Charlie whispered, his voice wavering. "So much I never thought I'd get to do because I'd never feel this way about someone else."

"So, I'm not imagining whatever this thing is, right?" I kept my arms wrapped around him, never wanting to let him go. "I promise you, this is not my usual when it comes to meeting people."

Charlie bit his lip. "Obviously same. What's your usual?"

We'd discussed our pasts a bit, but I got the feeling Charlie needed to talk and process in order to be comfortable with situations.

"I can't say I was ever trying very hard to meet the kind of guys looking for long-term, but I definitely wasn't finding any of them. I'd meet guys on dating apps from time-to-time and at bars, only rarely at work or a coffee shop. It never failed, I'd go into thinking maybe we'd date and get to know each other; he'd come into it thinking he'd found a big bear to fuck him silly before he sashayed away."

Charlie winced. "Yeah, that sucks. I think the whole issue of top or bottom has never really been something I've thought about very much because—even though I've thought about sex and got myself off—I've never really imagined sex with another person so positions or preferences in the bedroom haven't crossed my mind." He pursed his lips. "I know what I like, but I've never really considered it in relation to someone else being involved. If that makes sense."

"It does." I pressed a kiss over his cheek before brushing my lips over his. "Just to be open, I'm not against topping. I actually enjoy it. My issue has always been people just *assuming* I'm a strict top and never caring enough to ask or even care if it's what I wanted."

Charlie chewed on his lip. "But you like to bottom, too?"

My cock twitched and I wanted to drag Charlie up to my room. "Definitely."

"I think I want to try both," Charlie admitted with a rush of words followed by wide eyes and a sigh. "This is weird, right? It's so surreal to be talking to you about this stuff and feeling like I've known you my entire life. How does that even happen? I feel closer to you than even Stella and I've known her for ten some years. Don't get me wrong, I love her dearly and trust her completely, but there's something more with you than there's ever been with her." He ran a hand over his face. "And that's a very new situation for me. Even with the few guys I've made it to a second date with, I've never had the urge to think about sex with them. But with you? It's like I've known you since childhood and thinking about sex with you is the most natural thing in the world."

"That's good? Yeah?" I wasn't sure if Charlie had a point or he was just talking to help him process.

He nodded. "Very. Stella's always said I'd be bowled over one day when the right guy came along. I guess I've just never really thought it would happen." He shifted on the counter and wound his legs around me. "And now I'm a jumble of anxious anticipation and uncertain nerves all mixed with these sexual impulses I've never really had before."

I ran my hands up his torso, enjoying the heat of his skin under my touch, fighting the urge to bend and bite his pebbled nipples under the material of his soft shirt, and cupped his face in my hands. "Tonight. Anything you want to try, I'm down."

"Even if it's just handjobs or blowjobs?" Charlie's words told me he worried those acts wouldn't be enough for me.

"Always. *Sex* doesn't have to be penetration; not all people enjoy having fingers or a dick in their ass; not all people want to put their fingers or dick in an ass. Sex can be anything the people involved make it. If we didn't have guests arriving soon, I'm pretty sure we could take this far enough to claim we *had sex* on my kitchen counter because I'm seriously hard enough to hammer nails right now." I took his mouth gently, probing softly with my tongue, consuming his moans. "Tonight. And if you find you're not feeling it later, no big deal. I'm fine with popping in a movie and cuddling on the couch."

It wasn't just a line. The older I'd gotten, the more I'd realized a few things. One, sex was great, but it wasn't the end-all-be-all. Two, I'd rather have someone like Charlie to cuddle with than some random guy to fuck and leave. Three, I wanted to build something with the right guy.

My heart caught in my throat as I thought about how *right* things felt between Charlie and me.

"You don't think I'm just reacting this way because you're the first person to want to get to know me?" Charlie asked.

I shook my head. "You're an introvert in a lot of ways. You're demisexual. I'm not saying I'm some sort of unicorn, but based on what you've told me and what I've read, a guy could spend a year getting to know you and if you didn't feel a connection with him, you wouldn't have any kind of sexual attraction to him."

"You've been reading about being demisexual?" Charlie cocked his head, a soft smile filling his face.

I shrugged. "I wanted to know about what makes you you."

"That's really sweet." He pressed his lips to mine and I groaned when our tongues entwined, sending a jolt of lust straight to my cock.

We were interrupted by a knock at the front door.

"Our guests are here," Charlie said with a pout.

"First, I love that you're claiming them as *our guests* and two, thank you for being here. I want us to make friends and grow as individuals and…" I paused, giving Charlie a questioning look.

"What?"

"I was going to say *as a couple*, but I didn't know if that was too much, too soon," I said.

Charlie grinned and shook his head. "No, it's perfect. Knowing we're in something we both want to make work makes it even easier for me. Building on what we've already got, on this crazy pull between us, is showing me this is real even when it feels like it's too good to be true."

"Then, let's grow as individuals *and* as a couple. Starting with baked potatoes with our friends." I smacked a kiss against his lips and he hopped down from the counter.

The cats followed as we went to open the door for our friends.

SEVEN

CHARLIE

NIX: You won't believe what I just heard from Jo Ellen!

The text came through just as Otto's voice crackled over the radio. "Charlie, get your ass over here. Harley just told me some interesting news."

The baked potato bar the week before had been a success and our little group had promised to make it something of a weekly thing.

As much as I'd wanted to take things to the next level with Nix that night, Otto had stumbled upon getting home from his date and we'd ended up rushing to the cottage to check on him. Luckily, nothing had been broken and the bruise on his arm was healing nicely.

I'd been swamped with a deadline and Nix had picked up a new client, so we hadn't really seen each other much, but we had plans for dinner a bit later.

"Hold your horses," I said into the little two-way radio. "I'm on my way."

As I walked toward Otto's place, I texted Nix.

· · ·

Me: *Sorry, you texted right as Otto was demanding my presence. What's up?*

I'd learned Nix would only text if he wasn't with a client—similar to when I put my phone on silent when I was working—so the fact that he didn't reply wasn't surprising.

I popped my head into Otto's kitchen to find my uncle and Harley drinking coffee at the kitchen table. Otto was older than Harley, but they'd struck up a friendship and Harley came to visit two or three times a week. Sometimes Jo Ellen would be with him, but today he was on his own.

I poured myself a cup of coffee and sat down. "What's this interesting news?"

Otto was often giving me facts and tidbits he found entertaining or potentially promising for future book ideas. Sometimes his input proved to be useful, other times it was just funny shit. But I enjoyed visiting with my uncle, so I welcomed the break.

"Do you remember back when we first moved here and you said you thought it would be fun to own a little shop like Wayne's?" Otto asked, barely containing a grin.

"Yeah?"

He pointed to Harley. "Harley says it's on the downlow right now, but Jo Ellen heard from Wayne's wife they're moving down south to be closer to family and putting Wayne's on the market."

"No shit?" I asked, truly shocked. My phone buzzed again.

Nix: *I just heard from Jo Ellen that Wayne's is going up for sale.*

· · ·

Me: I'm hearing the exact same thing from Harley and Otto right this second.

My fingers trembled as I typed out the message. Glancing up to find Otto and Harley watching me, I gave a weak smile. "Nix was telling me the news."

"You want me to put in a good word? Get your name to Wayne as a potential buyer?" Harley asked.

My mind was racing a million miles a minute. "I don't know. Saying I wanted to own a place like that was one thing —a pipe dream. Actually doing it? I don't know that I could."

Harley gave an understanding smile. "Well, you think about it. I know Wayne would be happy to know the shop stays with locals instead of some enterprising young gun wanting to citify it or tear it down to build apartments."

My eyes went wide. "I'm not exactly a local." I frowned. "You really think that could happen if the wrong person buys it?"

Harley nodded. "I do. Wayne's grandson has been sniffing around for years and I know he definitely won't keep the shop the way it is."

I shook my head, disappointed in the thought. "Damn, I can't imagine doing that. But I honestly don't know if I could devote the time needed to run a place like Wayne's."

"But you said you had great ideas for improving on it," Otto argued.

"I do," I mused. "But that was before owning it was an actual reality."

"Well, I know for a fact that Jo Ellen will buy it before she lets it get changed too much or torn down. But she'd be happy to have you snatch it up," Harley said.

"You already have a writing schedule. You told me just the other day that you're between ghost contracts, it will be a while before you get edits back from your publisher, and you're making good progress on your self-pub work." Otto tapped the table. "You don't write *all* day, *every* day. Buy Wayne's, make your changes, use the people who already work there, figure out the times you can be on-site, and do your writing as usual. I don't want to see you give up on something you clearly want to do."

I smiled, but my mind was already in planning stage. Otto was right. The timing was perfect as far as fitting something other than writing into my schedule. I had money from Orson—and wouldn't he just hate the thought of his money going to help his oddball son buy a fabulous small-town grocery?

With a chuckle, I glanced between Otto and Harley. "You know what, go ahead and put in a word with Wayne; let him know I'm interested." With a grin, I amended, "*Very* interested."

We spent a few more minutes chatting, but Otto grinned and told me to get my ass home because he could tell I was distracted by the news about Wayne and my dinner date.

I gratefully rushed home and got ready for dinner, all the while running ideas and plans through my head—trying not to get *too* excited about a prospect that very likely wouldn't happen. I barely recalled the drive to the Chinese place, but I arrived home with just a few minutes to spare before my date arrived.

I bit back a giddy smile at the thought of having a *date* with someone I adored. Cricket and Hopper stared at me from their place on the kitchen window sill. I gave their ears a scratch. "Sorry, boys, I'm stupid excited about all of this."

The cats blinked and returned to watching out the window.

At six on the dot, Nix knocked on my backdoor.

Grinning like a fool, I opened the door and gasped. "Oh my God, they're gorgeous."

Nix handed me the most beautiful bouquet of flowers and leaned in to kiss my cheek. "So are you."

With a contented sigh, I wrapped my arms around his neck, the flowers poking at his head, and kissed him. Our tongues danced together and I knew I'd never experienced anything so right and perfect in my entire life.

"Hi," I whispered when we broke the kiss. "How was your day?"

"A bit rough. I think one of my clients may be moving toward needing more full-time care and I hate to see them upset about having to go to assisted living." Nix frowned.

"I'm sorry. I'm sure they'd much rather stay home and have you there."

He nodded, but I could tell he wasn't in the mood to chat about it much. "Are we eating here or going out?"

"Shhhh, don't tell Jo Ellen, but I ran out of town to grab Chinese," I whispered.

Nix laughed. "Your secret is safe. It's not like you're cheating on Briarton's Chinese restaurant since there *isn't* a Briarton Chinese restaurant."

"Right. That was my thought, exactly." I busied myself arranging the flowers in a vase while Nix grabbed the bag of take-out and began dishing up plates.

"So, I'm going to need you to talk about wanting to be millionaires," Nix said, his eyes gleaming.

"What?" I chuckled around an egg roll.

He waved a forkful of noodles my way. "You talked about wanting to own a place like Wayne's and *poof*, it's for sale. So, talk about us being millionaires so that can happen too." He grinned as he shoved the noodles in his mouth.

I chuckled. "I mean, I'm not going to tempt fate, so..."

Clearing my throat, I pretended to be speaking to the universe. "So, um, yeah, Mr. Universe? My friend Nix and I would *really* like to be millionaires. We'd do great things with the money, promise." I glanced at a grinning Nix and lowered my voice, my words more serious. "And, um, while we're on the topic of things we want, thanks for bringing this guy into my life."

Nix's entire face softened and he reached across the table for my hand, caressing his thumb over mine. "Just so we're clear, I'd take this over a million dollars any day," he whispered gruffly.

My heart nearly exploded and, just like that, I was gone.

Almost knocking over my chair, I stood and rounded the table, yanking Nix to stand. Slamming our mouths together, I laughed at Nix's grunt of surprise. "Food can wait," I mumbled against his mouth.

Nix groaned and maneuvered us toward the living room, pressing me onto the couch and fitting perfectly between my legs as he came down on top of me. He resumed the kiss, licking into my mouth, setting fire to my blood.

"God, Nix," I panted against his lips, "I'm terrified of fucking this up, but damn, I want to do so much."

Nix smiled and nuzzled my neck, rocking his hips into me. "Anything you want."

"I don't even know. Like I want to be naked and bent over the mattress for you right this very second, but I also know I should maybe move slower."

He chuckled. "Believe me, the feeling is *very* mutual. Probably a good thing we stopped at the couch. Just so you know, I'm ready and willing for whatever you're comfortable with—anytime, anyplace, you just say the word—but we'll go slow."

"I wanna touch you," I whispered, my voice catching as I imagined being naked with Nix.

"Can I undress you?" he asked, making my heart soar. I loved the way he so naturally wanted to be sure I was comfortable.

I nodded. "As long as you're getting naked, too."

Nix stood and stripped out of his clothes, his tall, broad, gorgeous body on display as I yanked my shirt over my head. Nix stilled my hands as I reached the button of my jeans. "Let me," he croaked out.

Moving my trembling hands from the button, I sighed as Nix trailed his hands from my collarbone, to my nipples, over the trail of hair on my belly, and finally paused on the waistband of my jeans. No longer able to keep my hands to myself, I reached for Nix and ran my hands up his big, strong arms and down his broad back, savoring the warmth of his skin and the tickle from the light dusting of hair under my palms.

My caressing hands reached his waist just as he popped the button on my jeans.

As he unzipped me, I teased my knuckles over his V-line.

When he shimmied me out of my pants and underwear, I lifted my hips just as my fingers trailed over his rock-hard cock.

As he gasped, I wrapped my fingers around him just as my own solid length slapped against my belly.

"Oh fuck, Charlie," Nix groaned, ducking his head to watch as I stroked him. "Fuck."

"Touch me," I begged, my cock leaking onto my abdomen.

Nix growled and moved his big hand between us, gripping my cock in his hot palm.

The whimper escaping me spurred us both on and we stroked each other, thumbing over our leaking slits as we rocked our hips and pressed our lips together in sloppy kisses.

Nix shifted, taking both of my hands and holding them

above my head as he rutted our erections together, making us both groan. "Fuck," he murmured, biting at my bottom lip and soothing the sting with his warm, wet tongue. "I could come just like this."

"Me, too," I gasped. "But not yet." I moved to sit up and pushed Nix to sit on the couch as I straddled his thick thighs. Grasping both our cocks in my hand, I began to stroke as I leaned forward and devoured Nix's mouth, thrusting my tongue between his lips like I wanted to thrust my cock into his ass.

Nix groaned and gripped my hand, joining me in stroking our cocks to completion. "You're so good," he murmured against my lips, "so fucking good."

We rocked our hips together, the warm friction from our hands and cocks driving us to release. "Oh fuck," I whimpered, "I'm gonna come."

"Do it," Nix commanded. "Tell me what you wanna do. Come for me."

With a grunt, I increased the stroking of our hands. "Wanna fuck you, feel your tight ass on my cock."

"God, yes," Nix moaned. "I'm gonna eat your ass and slide into your tight heat, wanna be inside you."

Our dirty talk pushed us both over the edge and our releases erupted between us, spilling over our knuckles and mixing together on Nix's stomach as we grunted and groaned.

"Holy fuck," I mumbled into Nix's neck when I'd finally caught my breath. "I know I only have a few kisses, porn, and my own hand to compare it to, but that was damn good on my side of things."

Nix chuckled. "I may have more experience, but I can assure you *that* was beyond damn good on my side of things."

I grinned against his sweaty skin. "Really?" It did crazy

things to my head and heart to think I was as good as Nix had ever had.

"One hundred percent truth. That was amazing." He used his clean hand to tip my chin and kiss me. "I feel so damn blessed we've built this thing between us and you're comfortable enough for this." He gestured to our spent cocks and the sticky mess. "What I feel for you is worth all the shitty hookups and disappointment in my past."

My eyes stung and my throat grew tight. "I'd truly given up on ever finding someone I could build enough of a connection with to experience this. I hate we both suffered and missed so much time together, but I'm grateful we found each other."

Nix kissed me again and smeared our release on his belly. "We need to clean up. And the food is probably cold." He glanced beyond me. "And the cats are watching. I think they're probably wondering what I just did to their daddy."

I snorted. "Cat pervs," I said as I looked toward the felines. They had the audacity to look bored as they licked their front paws, acting as if they hadn't just watched me shoot my load with a guy for the first time in my life.

We climbed from the couch, gathered our clothes, and padded to the bathroom to clean up.

"Will you stay here tonight?" I asked as we pulled on underwear.

Nix wrapped me in his arms. "If that's what you want. I'll have to run home in the morning to get ready for work and feed the cats, but tonight works."

I grinned into the kiss he pressed onto my lips before we headed to the kitchen to finish dinner.

Reheated Chinese had never tasted so good.

EIGHT

NIX

SLEEPING in Charlie's bed was something dreams were made of.

Not only had I done very little cuddling or *sleeping* with most of my past hookups—the majority didn't take place near a bed or the guy was itching for one of us to leave within moments of doing the deed—but, holding Charlie had immediately become something I wanted to do for the rest of my life.

He'd needed a little bit of time to adjust to me being in his bed, and we didn't stay pretzeled together the whole night, but Charlie's contented sighs against my chest told me he was just as happy with our little set-up as I was.

Just as the summer sun painted light pinks in the sky, I checked my phone.

We had an hour before I had to head home to get ready for work.

"What time is it?" Charlie grumbled.

"Early enough to make dreams come true," I whispered against his cheek with a smile, loving the rough prickle of his unshaven jaw under my lips.

"Mmmm," Charlie hummed, thrusting his ass into me. "Well, not enough time for *certain* dreams, but I've gone without for this long, I can make do," he teased.

We'd slept in just our underwear and I thumbed his waistband. "Can we get rid of these?"

He rolled to his back and stripped the material down his legs, kicking the article of clothing somewhere out of view. "You're overdressed," he told me with a smirk as he lazily stroked his cock.

I made quick work of my own underwear and gripped my erection. "What do you want?"

"Wanna suck you," Charlie said with heat in his eyes. "And feel your mouth on me."

"You name the position," I said, knowing everything we were doing was new for Charlie and wanting him to be comfortable.

"Sit on my chest," he said.

I groaned and straddled him, my balls resting against the soft skin of his upper chest. My leaking cock bobbed, brushing Charlie's chin. "This what you want?" I fisted my cock and tapped the swollen head against his lips.

Charlie flicked his tongue out to lap up my precum, his eyes never leaving mine.

Gripping my cock, I dropped my head back, savoring the wet heat of my lover's tongue on my cock.

Returning my gaze to Charlie's face, I groaned as he took me between his lips and swirled his tongue around my cock head. "Fuck, Charlie."

He smiled the best he could with his mouth full of my dick and took me the rest of the way in, gagging slightly when I hit the back of his throat, my balls pressing on his chin.

Charlie pulled from my cock and, for a moment, I worried something was wrong. But he licked his lips and said, "Don't go easy. I won't break." He opened his mouth again and took me deep, reaching behind to tease his finger up and down my ass, brushing gently over my hole with each pass.

Knowing Charlie didn't want *easy* allowed me to grip the headboard and fuck into his mouth, loving the slick, wet heat engulfing my cock.

As Charlie teased my entrance and gripped my hip, I fell into the perfect rhythm and all too soon my orgasm was threatening. When his finger pressed into me just slightly, I gave a final thrust and shot my release onto his tongue with a loud groan.

Moving from Charlie's chest, I flopped on top of him and kissed him, loving the taste of me on his tongue. "I need your dick in my mouth, stat."

"Mmmm, love when you use medical terms," Charlie teased. "Can I stay like this?"

I rolled from his body and reached for his rock-hard cock. "This okay?"

He nodded and spread his legs as I stroked him.

"Bend your knees and thrust into my mouth," I instructed before moving to lick him like a lollipop and take his length deep into my mouth. After the first taste, I slicked my fingers with spit and teased his tight pucker as I took his cock back between my lips.

Charlie whimpered and tensed.

"You okay? Want me to stop?" I asked.

"I'm good. Keep going." Charlie rolled his hips, taking his cock in hand and directing it back to my mouth. "Suck me, please."

We found a satisfying rhythm of Charlie thrusting, my head bobbing up and down, and my finger teasing open his tight hole. When I pushed my middle finger inside and pressed my thumb against his taint, Charlie's cock exploded on my tongue, pulsing his hot load deep in my throat as he cried out.

Charlie hissed as I licked at his spent cock. "Too much," he said. "Sorry."

"Don't be sorry, we have to let each other know what we like." I shifted so I could pull him into my arms. "You okay?"

"That was amazing. I feel like a kid who just discovered how much fun roller coasters are and I want to ride them over and over and over," Charlie mumbled against my chest.

"We can make that happen. Just have to be sure we've lined up the tickets, the weather is good, and you don't mind lines," I teased.

Charlie popped his head up. "Are those metaphors? If so, I'm not following at all."

I smirked. "No, I was just trying to stick to the roller coaster theme, but I'm not as creative as you. I'm just saying, we can totally do everything you want to do." I kissed him. "And even if last night and this morning is all you ever want to do, it's enough." Tipping up his chin, I kissed him, slower and deeper. "I'm not in this just for sex, Charlie. This is very real to me."

He nodded, his eyes suspiciously bright. "Same for me. I used to wonder if I'd ever just find someone I might feel comfortable enough with to at least settle into some sort of domestic partnership as close friends—even if the sexual attraction wasn't there—because that's what I want. I want a partnership, a friendship, someone to share my life with."

"You've got it," I murmured against his lips. "Sex or no sex, this thing between us is something special."

"But the sex is good, right?" Charlie pulled back and studied me. "You're not like trying to tell me I should focus my skills elsewhere because I suck?"

I chuckled and nuzzled his jawline. "Oh, you *suck* all right," I teased. "Very well, in fact."

"Oh my God, that was almost as bad as an Otto sex joke." Charlie groaned and then palmed his face. "Oh my God, I'm talking about my uncle after sex. That's so wrong."

I laughed and slapped his ass. "Get this pretty ass out of bed. We'll get ready and walk to Piping Hot for coffee before work."

"You have time?" Charlie asked.

"Yep, if we hurry, we can get coffee and say goodbye from there." I stood and pulled on last night's clothes. "Hope Otto doesn't see me doing the walk of shame back home."

Charlie snorted. "He'd probably cheer you on."

I smacked a kiss against his lips. "Twenty minutes. Meet me on the sidewalk."

He rolled from the bed and stood, his naked body on display making me want to cancel all appointments for the day and drag him back to bed. "Twenty minutes. I'll be there. Put your order in on the app so we don't have to wait."

We met up exactly twenty minutes later, me in my scrubs and Charlie in his joggers and a form-fitting t-shirt. He looked damn good in anything he had on—and in nothing at all—but the uber casual clothes he wore for writing were downright sizzling. How a man could make joggers and a t-shirt look sexy, I'd never know, but Charlie did it with ease.

"Why are you staring?" he asked.

"Just thinking about how hot you look in casual-wear."

Charlie snorted. "I look like a bum. People who don't know what I do probably think I'm the biggest couch potato and don't even own any dressy clothes."

"Do you?"

"Own dressier clothes? Yeah. I have a couple suits. I'm not one to get fancy, but I *can* pull out the jeans and a decent shirt for something involving more than just a dinner in my kitchen."

"I like you in whatever you wear. Always," I assured him.

"Same," Charlie agreed. "But I gotta say that your ass in scrubs is the stuff my dreams are made of."

"Oh, really?" I teased. "Good to know and definitely noted." I bumped into him as we started down the sidewalk. "I like knowing you've checked out my ass."

"It's a nice ass."

"Thanks, I grew it myself."

Charlie chuckled. "I kinda like knowing you think I'm hot in joggers."

"Mmm, that I do. I'm thinking about getting you a pair of light grey ones as a gift. Grey sweatpants..." I paused to bite my knuckles, pretending to grasp for control, "they *do* things for me."

"I've got a pair. I'll wear them sometime, just for you." Charlie's cheeks pinked, but I could tell he liked having me gush about how hot I thought he was.

"You're too good to me."

As we walked toward Piping Hot, our fingers brushed. Taking a chance, I took Charlie's hand and gave it a squeeze. "This okay?"

He smiled and squeezed back. "Yeah."

"So, we didn't really talk much about it. What are you thinking about Wayne's going up for sale?" I asked, adjusting my work bag on my shoulder.

Charlie sucked air through his teeth with a cute little grin. "I told Harley to put in a good word for me and let Wayne know I'm *very* interested."

"Yeah? That's great."

His brows drew together. "Is it? I mean, it's something I've always thought would be fun, but that was in theory, not actuality. Am I crazy to think I can keep up with my writing *and* own a small-town grocery? The *entire* town relies on Wayne's to keep them supplied with food and whatnot. Can I fill those shoes?"

We'd reached Piping Hot and the place was packed as usual. "Hold that thought. You wanna grab that table," I pointed to the one empty spot open in the outside patio area, "and I'll grab our orders?"

Once I returned with our coffees, I sat in the chair nearest Charlie and dove back into the conversation. "I don't know your schedule *exactly*, but I know you often say you can't write for hours a day and you need a break. I think you said you were taking a small pause on the ghost writing and it will be a while until you get edits back from your publisher. Right now, I think the self-pub is all you're working on." I sipped my drink. "Owning the grocery wouldn't mean you have to work there all day, every day."

"True." Charlie nodded. "Otto said I could keep the people who already work there, make my improvements as needed, and use the new venture as a break from writing." He took a drink. "I find myself getting bored when I'm not writing, but sometimes there just aren't any words left for the day. Having the store would be something productive outside of writing."

I took his hand. "Or you could read, nap, paint, whatever during your downtime. I don't want you to think you *have* to jump into owning a business."

Charlie smiled and sighed. "I know. But it's something I've always wanted. I just didn't realize it would be something actually within my reach. I think I'll go for it; if it doesn't happen, it doesn't happen."

"Well, I'll be here to help as much as possible."

His eyes widened. "You will?"

I squeezed his hand. "Of course. If you want your boyfriend there to help, I'll be there to help."

Charlie glanced at our hands and back up to me. "Oh my God, I have a boyfriend." He pressed his lips together, biting back a goofy grin. "This little town is magical or something.

Obviously, I want you there." Then he frowned. "Do you think I can handle the social aspect of owning a business?"

"Yeah, I do. You've been in town and getting to know people. You're more at ease now than when we first met. I think you can handle it." I took the last drink of my coffee. "Plus, you don't *have* to talk to every customer. That's why you'll have a schedule of when you're there and when you're not so you don't get overwhelmed."

Charlie nodded. "You're right. I'm going to do it. Fingers crossed I haven't just gotten my hopes up for nothing." He finished his drink and we stood.

After tossing our cups in the trash, we walked down the sidewalk, hand-in-hand. "I see Otto today, he's my last appointment of the day. You wanna do dinner with the three of us tonight?"

"Sounds good." Charlie was quiet for a moment. "Does Dr. Pierce know we're dating? Is that a problem since my uncle is one of your patients?"

"No. I told him about us. If *you* were my patient, that would be different. It's all good." We reached the end of the block where Charlie needed to go left and I needed to go right for my first appointment. "Have a good day. L...let me know how things go with the store." My heart skipped a beat. I'd nearly said *love you*.

Charlie gave me a quizzical look before brushing a kiss over my cheek. "You, too. See you this evening."

I examined the near-miss on the way to Ms. Molly's house. Did I love Charlie? We hadn't known each other long, but I knew without a doubt he was the person I'd been waiting for my entire life. Charlie made me happy, made me look forward to the future, and had me floating on air in a way no other person *ever* had.

Yeah, I loved Charlie.

Strangely enough, the realization didn't freak me out.

Instead, I had a huge smile on my face as I rang Ms. Molly's doorbell.

"Well, look at you all smiley this morning," she said in greeting when she opened the door.

"Good morning. You ready for your appointment?" I was taking her to Dr. Pierce for some routine blood work and an exam.

"Yes, sir. Grateful you can drive me. Let's get going." Molly grabbed her purse and handed me the keys. "I'm not a fan of blood work, but it's a beautiful morning and I'm happy to be out of the house."

We drove the short distance to Dr. Pierce's office and I parked as close to the door as possible. The next few moments happened so fast, yet they played out like a nightmare in slow motion. Before I could even get out of the car and around to the passenger side, Molly had somehow managed to get out, take fewer than three steps, and trip over the curb. The poor lady had bloodied her hands something fierce and chunks of mulch stuck to her raw skin.

"Well, shit," Molly exclaimed, her voice pinched in pain as I rushed to her side. "That wasn't supposed to happen."

I assessed the situation and determined she hadn't hit her head and she wasn't in enough pain for anything big to be broken. Molly assured me she was bruised and the scrapes on her hands hurt "like the dickens," but she didn't feel like anything was severely damaged.

A nurse, who must have seen the fall from the office window, appeared with a wheelchair. Molly grumbled about it, but she settled in and let me push her inside.

We took her straight to a room and Dr. Pierce met us.

"Well, Ms. Molly, it looks as if you've had some excitement," he said as he checked her chart while the other nurse and I cleaned Molly's hands. "If you're okay with it, I'd like to get you cleaned up and bandaged and go ahead with the blood work and exam. We can postpone, but I'd hate for you to have to make another trip."

Molly, bless her soul, sat there with her hands dripping pink as we wiped away the water and leveled a very serious gaze at the doctor. "Yeah, I'd hate to take another *trip*," she deadpanned.

Dr. Pierce smirked and shook his head. "My bad. Let's get you taken care of and Nixon can get you back home to rest. I want to x-ray those wrists; a tumble like you took isn't good on bones."

Molly started to protest, but I patted her shoulder. "Just a precaution. Might as well do it while we're here."

"I feel like a fool, falling like that," she grumbled.

"I feel like a heel for not being there to help," I answered with a squeeze to her shoulder. Truly, the fall could have been much worse and I hated to think about it. In reality, the fall wasn't my fault, but I still felt horrible she'd gotten hurt.

"Nonsense, I know better than to try to navigate curbs and such without help these days. I just appreciate you being there to help me up."

While Molly was wheeled away for her x-rays, exam, and bloodwork, I spent a bit of time working on paperwork.

A couple hours later, I had Molly settled on her couch with some pain relievers, water, and her remote. The trip to Dr. Pierce, her unexpected injuries, and all that followed had worn her out. I knew she'd take a nice long nap. I left with the promise to call her a bit later.

I spent the rest of my day doing my normal tasks and chatting with patients. Not only did I love my job because I was helping people, but I enjoyed getting to spend time with some really amazing folks who had years and years of stories to tell.

By the time I got to Otto's place, I was ready to call it a day and switch from nurse mode to Nix mode. Unfortunately, it was the day for injuries and Otto met me with a grumpy and pained expression.

"What's up?" I asked, assessing the situation.

"Did something to my damn finger," he grumbled, holding up us hand. "And I wasn't even using it for anything fun. Tried picking up my box of records but pain shot through my finger and it's been throbbing ever since."

"Let's get all the usual taken care of and then we'll take a look at the finger," I said and set to work with routine vitals and questions.

As much as he groused about it, Otto did a good job sticking to his medication routine and eating as healthy as possible. I knew he snuck some treats in here and there and I didn't blame him.

When I finished my notes, I took Otto's hand and examined the finger. "It's slightly swollen. I'm thinking a sprain more than likely. *Possibly* a stress fracture, but that's not my first thought. I'm going to wrap it and we'll let it heal for a bit—either way, treatment is the same. Wrap it, ice it, elevate it, let it rest. No fun times for that hand for a while." I worked to wrap his index finger to his middle finger.

"How the hell am I supposed to jack off?" Otto asked.

I snorted. "Use your other hand." I taped off the wrap.

"Can't flip anyone the bird this way."

"Use your other hand." I couldn't help but grin at his grumpy expression.

Otto raised his left hand and flipped me off. "Gonna have to see if I can get anyone to come over and take care of things for me."

I scowled. "You know Charlie and I will help with whatever you need. You shouldn't be doing a bunch of housework anyway." *Charlie and I* had so easily become part of my daily thoughts and vocabulary.

The old man snorted. "Wasn't talkin' about *chores* and I

sure as hell don't want you or my nephew getting your hands or mouths anywhere close to my junk."

I scoffed. "When we first met, you went on and on about being happy to have me doing your prostate exam," I mused. "Oh, how things have changed."

"That was before I knew you wanted to bone Charlie. Or be boned by him. Or both." Otto shook his head. "I can get kinky, but not with my nephew and his boyfriend."

My brows shot up and Otto smirked.

"Mmhm, I heard from a very happy little bird today that my nephew has a boyfriend."

I bit my lip, trying not to grin like a fool. "What a coincidence, I seem to have a new boyfriend as well."

Otto chuckled. "You boys are good for each other. Treat him right."

"Always," I promised, meaning the word with every fiber of my being. "Charlie and I were planning dinner, you coming?"

"Nah, my finger hurts. Think I'd rather listen to some records and maybe watch some movies before just heading to bed." He leaned in close. "Don't tell my home health nurse, but I've got some pain medication to knock me out."

I frowned. "No, you don't. Charlie and I cleaned out your medicine cabinet a while back."

"Damn it, how am I supposed to sleep now?"

I cocked my head. "Those pills were beyond old. I'll give you some over-the-counter pain medication and something to help you sleep. If the pain is worse tomorrow, we can talk about a prescription pain killer, but medication like that can wreak havoc on your bowel movements."

Otto grunted. "Just give me what you've got. I'd rather poop and just deal with the pain."

Otto was falling right in line with my theory that every year of age made a person more and more vested in having a well-working digestive system and satisfying bowel movements.

"What are you going to eat? Want us to bring you something over?" I handed him two pain relievers and a bottle of water. "These other two plus the sleep-aid can be taken in four to six hours."

Otto nodded. "Don't worry about my dinner. I've got some soup I can warm up."

I checked to see the baby monitor unit was turned on, volume up, and nestled up high enough Otto couldn't get to it for the batteries—even though it plugged in, Charlie had advised not leaving it where Otto could filch the batteries in case of a power outage. "You holler if you need anything. We're eating at Charlie's tonight." I moved Otto's box of records and the record player closer to his chair.

"Just make sure the two-way radio isn't on. I don't need to hear the two of you going at it reminding me of what I'm *not* doing tonight."

I laughed, trying not to think about what Charlie and I could possibly do later that night. "You still have your left hand."

"You ever jack off with your opposite hand? It's like running a race with your shoe laces tied together," Otto grumbled.

"Best you just get some rest tonight anyway." I packed up my bag and headed toward the door. "Call out or text if you need anything."

Otto flipped me a left-handed middle finger and turned toward his record player.

I made my way through the backyard to my house and tossed my bag on the counter before grabbing a bottle of water and flopping down on the couch. CoJack and Cheddar immediately came to greet me with meows and purrs. The day had knocked me out and I wanted nothing more than to eat dinner and spend time with Charlie. Which was proof of how I'd changed as I'd gotten older. Younger me would have been itching to go out, have fun, find a hook-up that would maybe possibly—even though deep down I knew it wouldn't —turn into something more.

Now, all I wanted was to enjoy a quiet—maybe steamy— evening with my boyfriend and get a decent night of sleep.

I snorted at myself, but I wasn't disappointed. Honestly, I liked myself and my life a whole lot more at forty-five than I ever did in my twenties and thirties.

My phone buzzed twice.

First was a text from an old friend back in the city telling me he was going to be driving through the area and asking if we could meet up. I responded quickly to let him know that would be great and to just let me know general dates and times.

The second was from Charlie telling me to come over whenever I was ready.

Just as I started to reply, another text from Charlie came through.

Charlie: Feel free to interpret "ready" in whatever way you want, but your boyfriend might feel like doing something new tonight.

My mouth hit the floor and my cock grew *very* interested.

Charlie: I mean, only if that's something you might want.

I smiled. Charlie freak out in three, two, one...

Charlie: Oh God, why can't you unsend texts? I'm dying. Forget I said anything. Get ready however you want to get ready. I probably wouldn't even be very good at topping.

I groaned at the image of Charlie inside me. I knew exactly what my *getting ready* before dinner was going to entail.

Charlie: Never mind. Forget dinner. I'm not available because I've died of embarrassment. I'm very sorry for your loss.

I laughed out loud and thumbed in a reply.

Me: *I'm so on board. Stop texting me so I can "get ready." I'm hungry—for food and for you, so prepare yourself.*

Adding a winky face and kissy face, I hit send and headed to the bathroom. A nice long shower and thorough prepping was just what I needed to clear the weight of my day. Looking forward to time with Charlie had me more excited about something than I'd been in a very long time.

Sure, the idea of sex was great, but just holding him and talking to him was enough to have me grinning like a fool and dancing around the bathroom in anticipation.

I wasn't sure what I'd done to deserve a great job, a fabulous home in a fantastic little town, and falling in love with the man of my dreams, but I wasn't going to take it for granted.

NINE

CHARLIE

BEFORE I COULD DIE of embarrassment *or* anticipation, my phone rang.

"Hello?"

"Hi, Charlie Hillion?"

"Yes," I said.

"This is Wayne Maxwell. I was just speaking to Harley and Jo and they told me you might be interested in buying the grocery from me."

My heart lodged in my throat. "Yes, sir. Owning a small business has always been something I've wanted to do."

"Well, I tell ya what, I don't have the time or inclination to hem-haw around. The wife and I are needed down south to help with a fragile pregnancy and two rambunctious two-year-old twins. I'd prefer to skip putting the place on the market and vetting potential buyers."

"Understandable, sir. I'm sorry to hear of your family issues. Well wishes for mother and baby."

"Thank you, son. Listen, I've spoken in depth to Harley and Jo and they've both sung your praises to Heaven and back. Morgan and Justin are respectable businessmen and members of this community and they can't say enough good things about you and your uncle."

"Thank you, sir, that's nice to hear." I wasn't exactly sure where he was going with this conversation, but my heart soared to hear my new friends had spoken so highly of me.

"I'd like to name a price. If it's something you can work with, let's get the papers drawn up and the sale finalized. Does that work for you?"

My stunned silence must have made Wayne think I wasn't sure.

"We've been in the black all but the first year of business so I assure you you'll be taking over a thriving business," he said. "Most of my employees have been working for me at least ten years and they could run the place with their eyes closed. You can make changes you think are for the best, even change the name if you think it needs changed, but the store almost runs itself. Are you interested?"

After nearly choking on my own tongue, I sputtered out something resembling a *yes*.

Wayne gave me the price point he was looking for.

I calculated what money I had from Orson and in my own savings. It was totally doable. "That's a workable price," I said. Back in the city, there was no way I could have afforded to pay upfront for a shop like Wayne's, but things were different in Briarton.

"Can we meet tomorrow and get the paperwork signed?" Wayne asked. "I hate to put a rush on it, but my wife's heading south at the end of the week and I'd like to go with her instead of following later."

"Yes, sir, I understand. Let me contact my bank about accessing my money." I glanced at the clock on the stove. "They're closed for the day. Can we make it the day after so I've had time to get my financial situation squared away?"

"We can make that work. Let's meet here at the store so I

can introduce you and show you around. Marla has been taking care of orders for years now, so she'll keep that going; you won't have to worry about things running smoothly. If you want to change or add something, just talk to Marla." He cleared his throat. "Of course, it'll be your place, so you won't answer to anyone. But Marla is a good, trustworthy worker."

"Understood, sir. I'll see you day after tomorrow at the store. How's nine?"

"Perfect. See you then." Wayne disconnected the call.

I stared at the phone and replayed the entire conversation, looking for any warning signs or red flags.

Wayne's wouldn't have been a staple of Briarton for over two decades if it wasn't a solid business.

Harley and Jo Ellen wouldn't have been so keen on me buying the place if it wasn't a sound investment.

Morgan and Justin wouldn't have encouraged me to take the leap if it wasn't a good idea.

Nothing had me worried about the actual purchase—I knew I'd make back my cost plus some as long as I kept the store running smoothly. The new ideas I had could wait for a bit, but I had a feeling adding just a few things—with help from locals—would make Wayne's an even bigger draw than it already was.

As far as my issues with socializing, I'd found I was more comfortable in Briarton than back in the city. Down here, it was easier to get to know people. I didn't think there were many people in town I didn't at least recognize and most I knew by face and name. I wouldn't *have* to chat with every single customer, but I would definitely do my damned best to keep the grocery business focused on our little town rather than forcing people to buy from the big discount shops.

Local was where it was at and I planned to keep it that way.

I pulled myself from my head as best I could and headed to the kitchen to feed the cats. As they meowed and rubbed against my legs like they hadn't been fed all damn day, I thought about Nix's text.

He was hungry? For me. *Prepare yourself.*

I knew what I'd been insinuating to him. Was he indicating the same back to me? Damn, this shit was hard. We needed to just talk about it, be upfront, but I didn't mind the flirty, suggestive texts.

I left the cats to eat and rushed upstairs to shower and get ready.

I wasn't one hundred percent sure where the night was headed, but I wanted to be comfortable in the fact I was prepared just in case.

Due to my curiosities—I wasn't turned off by sex, just the idea of sex with someone I didn't feel a strong connection with—I knew what I was doing as far as *getting ready*. I took care of all pertinent steps and finished off with a nice hot shower, the entire time thinking about how happy I was to have Nix coming over.

Scratch that.

How happy I was in general.

My writing was going well. I loved my new home and the quaint town we'd landed in. I was settling in with new friends. Otto was doing great. I was soon going to own a little dream I never really thought would come true. *And* I'd met a man I'd truly come to accept didn't exist until that fateful day in Piping Hot when we reached for the same coffee.

Fate definitely had her hand in the mix and she'd done some amazing things with location and timing. As I wiped off the steamy mirror, I smiled. Maybe it had taken forty-five years for me to get to this place in my life, but I was here now and I never wanted to take any of it for granted.

Nix was on the kitchen floor playing with the cats when I came downstairs. Like a big kid in his happy place, he looked up at me with the most gorgeous smile and it hit me like a punch to the solar plexus. I was in love with him.

I knew what love felt like. I loved Otto. I loved Stella.

But I'd never be *in love*.

One look at my big, blond teddy bear cuddling on the floor with my boys and I knew right then and there what it felt like to be in love.

Crossing the kitchen floor, I reached for his hand and pulled him up to stand, wrapping my arms around him, and devouring his mouth.

Nix didn't miss a beat, lifting me and placing my ass on the island counter as he pushed my legs apart and stepped close, never slowing the kiss.

When we finally broke for air, I couldn't help but smile as we pressed our foreheads together.

"That was a greeting I could get used to," Nix said, thumbing my bottom lip.

"I love you," I blurted. For a split second, I thought about trying to retract the words, make an excuse for saying them, pretend I wasn't serious. But the way Nix's pretty blue eyes sparkled brightly, I realized I didn't *want* to pretend the words had been a mistake. "I saw you sitting there, playing with my cats, waiting for me, and it hit me like a ton of bricks. I love you. I'm *in love* with you."

Before I could let him know it was okay if he didn't feel the same, Nix laughed and kissed me. Hard and slow, exploring my mouth and setting fire to my veins. When he pulled away, eyes full of desire, he chuckled. "I love you, too. Almost said it today, but freaked myself out about possibly freaking you out." He placed soft kisses all over my face. "You are the man I'd given up on ever finding. It took a lot longer than I ever wanted it to, but I wouldn't trade what we've got now for the world."

With stinging eyes and a bubble of laughter escaping my lips, I cupped his face. "Just when I'd finally accepted I'd probably never find a man I could actually connect with and build a real relationship, you came along and tried to steal my coffee."

Nix laughed and leaned his face into my palm.

"I agree it kind sucks it took us this long to find each other, but I see it as fate making sure everything was perfect before we met. Perfect location, perfect situation, perfect timing." I sighed into Nix's warm embrace.

"Not sure I've ever gotten anything perfect in my life," he whispered gruffly, "until you."

"Food and chat first? Or bedroom?" I asked, biting my lip.

Nix groaned. "How is that even a choice?"

But then his stomach rumbled.

I laughed. "So, food?"

"How about we pregame, eat, then head upstairs?" Nix waggled his brows.

"Pregame?" I asked and then yelped as Nix picked me up and headed toward the living room.

He put me down. "I can't eat and chat while wanting to suck you. We get off first, then we can have a nice, civilized, non-horny dinner while we talk about our days. *Then*, we can spend the rest of the night doing whatever feels right."

"Perfect," I said as I yanked my shirt over my head. "I was thinking pizza and beer for dinner. Is that okay?"

"Yep, but I want my appetizer first," he growled as he bent to take my nipple between his teeth.

In a flurry of lips, teeth, tongues, and hands we somehow got ourselves naked and onto the couch. Before I could decipher whose mouth was going where first, Nix rolled us from the couch to the floor with an oomph.

As I laughed, he maneuvered our bodies into a sixty-nine position and gripped my cock. My laughing died and I grunted with a thrust of my hips. Nix took me deep into his warm, wet mouth as I nuzzled my nose into the thatch of dark blond hair at the base of his shaft. Breathing in deeply, I savored the scent of soap and Nix, before cupping his balls and sucking one between my lips. Nix moaned around my cock and I lost any pretense of trying to drag out the blow job. I needed him in my mouth like I needed my next breath. His lips and tongue were doing wicked things to my dick and I knew I wouldn't last long.

Appreciating the fact I'd finally, *finally* connected with someone I wanted to have sex with—the fact I'd gone and fallen in love with him when I'd often wondered if that was even in the cards for me—I flicked my tongue over Nix's leaking cock head and enjoyed the salty bitter explosion of flavor.

"Suck me," Nix begged, his hot breath teasing over my throbbing, ready-to-explode cock.

With a slight thrill coursing through my body at his demand, I took him deep and moaned. Nix returned to sucking me and we filled the room with grunts, groans, and wet, sloppy sex noises. When he fondled my balls and a tingle built at the base of my spine, I increased my thrusts and my sucking. Nix grew harder in my mouth and I reached to tease a finger between his ass cheeks, playing with his hole.

In response, Nix spread my ass and tapped his finger against my hole as he bobbed his head up and down, taking my cock to the back of his throat. When he gripped my shaft and stroked along with his mouth, I lost it. An orgasm crashed over me as my release shot hot and heavy onto his tongue.

Groaning around the thick cock still stretching my lips

open, I reached to jerk Nix's dick once, twice, three times before he was unloading deep in my mouth.

We collapsed, breathing hard as we wiped our mouths and chins.

"Oh my God, we're never having sex here again," Nix grumbled. "Get your cats their own porn subscription or something."

I opened an eye to peek around the room as Nix sat up and yanked me into his arms. Laughing, I saw both Cricket and Hopper staring at us as if we were both ridiculous and boring. "I'm sorry, they've never experienced their daddy getting his brains sucked out. They're concerned."

Nix snorted. "They don't look concerned. They look bored and judgmental."

"They totally do." I grabbed a tissue from the box next to the couch and cleaned my belly and hand before handing it to Nix.

"I don't even get a new one?" he teased.

"You just had my cock in your mouth and your finger nearly in my ass, I didn't think a slightly used tissue would be a problem." I slapped a hand against his chest. "Let's get dressed and order the pizza. The beer is already cold."

We paused long enough to savor a slow, sensual kiss chock full of promises for *later* before pulling on our clothes.

By that time, the cats had retreated to their tree and Nix chuckled. "Pervy cats; the show's over, so they're gone."

"Part two will be behind closed doors." I kissed him, loving the way he naturally held me close. "I'd hate for you to get performance anxiety."

Nix slapped my ass and kissed me hard. "I love you," he murmured against my mouth when we finally came up for air.

"I love you." Feeling as if I was in an alternate universe, I sighed and let him hold me for a bit longer. "Can you start a fire outside and I'll call for the pizza?"

Thirty minutes later, after we'd checked in on Otto and had two beers apiece, we settled in with our pizza as the fire warmed the patio. We were smack in the middle of summer, but the day had been somewhat cooler than average and the evening was beyond pleasant.

"So, was Otto as charming with you today as he was this evening?" I asked with a smirk around a bite of gooey cheese.

Nix snorted. "He's in pain and it's definitely affecting his normally delicate personality."

"Delicate is the last word I'd ever use for that man," I said. "You think he'll be okay?"

"Yeah, I think it's a sprain. Even if it's a stress fracture, the treatment is the same. He's mostly mad because he can't give people the bird or jack off."

I nearly choked on my beer. "He said that? Dear Lord. Guess he'll have to use his other hand."

"That's what I told him, but he mentioned something about jacking off with his opposite hand being like running a race with his shoelaces tied together." Nix took a long swallow of beer and I couldn't help the way my eyes traveled down his throat. "But he definitely managed to flip me off with his other hand."

"How was the rest of your day?"

"Well, Otto was the end of a long day." Nix launched into a story about Ms. Molly and her fall.

I took his hand as he finished, knowing he felt guilty. "It wasn't your fault. You didn't know she was going to get out and try to do it all herself."

He shrugged. "I should have told her to sit still or something."

"If she's anything like Otto, she wouldn't have taken

kindly to that and likely wouldn't have done it anyway. I'm sure she doesn't blame you."

"No, she blames herself. I just feel bad she got hurt on my watch." Nix boxed up the remainder of the pizza. "I know she's embarrassed and hates that she fell. It's not easy getting old. She's the kindest, most grateful person I've ever met, but I know she gets down that she can't drive, can't step up on a curb, can't live completely on her own. She's great for her age, but that doesn't make it any easier. I'm sure it weighs on her mind that a lot of her friends have moved to assisted living. She's kinda stuck between a rock and a hard place; she likes having the independence she still has, but she misses her friends." Nix finished off his beer. "I think I may talk to her and her daughter about maybe visiting friends at one of the nearby facilities from time-to-time."

I nodded and took a final drink from my bottle. "She'd probably like that. Get to see her friends *and* kinda get used to what a place like that is like. Maybe it would help her see it's not terrible." We picked up our plates and napkins and carried everything into the kitchen. "I know Otto is convinced assisted living facilities are the devil, but he's never been to one."

Nix put the pizza in the fridge and washed the counter while I threw away our trash. "Yeah, I think a lot of people his age picture assisted living as a nursing home—don't get me wrong, nursing homes play an important part and often get a bad rap. Although, they aren't usually the most pleasant places to be, but not all of them are bad. Assisted living isn't a death sentence, but it's hard for older folks to understand that. A lot of them have friends who go to assisted living and they never see them again—sure, maybe those friends end up in nursing homes several years later at the end of their lives, but Otto and Molly don't see that part. They just know their friends went to assisted living and then they passed away—doesn't matter it may have been years later."

I wrapped my arms around Nix's broad shoulders. "I think the thought of being made to give up independence is probably terrifying to a lot of people. Molly's lost her husband and her ability to drive, she's lost friends, thinking about losing the last of her independence has to be unsettling."

Nix sighed. "Yeah, for sure. I just want to make their remaining independent years as enjoyable and healthy as possible. Days like today are just hard." He nuzzled my neck. "It's even harder when I lose a patient. It doesn't happen as often in this position, but it sucks when it does. I'll do my best not to bring shit home with me, but sometimes it's unavoidable."

I tipped his chin. "I'd be concerned if you *didn't* bring it home—if you *weren't* bothered by it. You work with some amazing folks. I'll be devastated when we lose Otto, it only makes sense you'd feel the same about your clients."

Nix pressed his forehead to mine. "I love you. Not just because you listen and let me talk through things, but it's amazing how good it feels to have someone to tell all this shit to."

"I'm always willing to listen. Even if I can't fix anything, I'll always listen."

We stood in a warm, silent embrace for several moments, just enjoying the contact.

"Tell me about your day," Nix said.

I couldn't hide the grin as I told him about the call with Wayne.

"That's amazing," Nix said, smacking a kiss to my lips. "I'm so excited for you."

We chatted a bit about the call I needed to make to the bank the next day, the first few changes I wanted to make—

not really *changes*, just additions—and why I wanted to sit down and talk with Morgan and Justin about our businesses so we could support each other and not become competition.

"I'm done talking about the shop for a while," I murmured against Nix's ear. "I believe you promised a main event after dinner?"

"First one to the bedroom gets to call the position," Nix whispered before laughing and running toward the stairs.

I yelped at the unfair advantage and took off after him.

We pushed and shoved and yelled—all in good fun—as we made our way up the stairs. Nix started stripping out of his clothes before he even reached the bedroom door and I couldn't help but laugh at his antics.

"Winner," he exclaimed, his arms held high over his head as he stood next to the bed in all his naked glory.

Not wanting to be left out, and longing to feel his bare body against me, I shucked my own clothes and kicked the door shut before stepping closer. "Not sure there are any losers in this situation," I whispered, biting my lip as our plump cocks nestled together.

Nix's arms came around me and pulled me close, kissing me breathless as he pushed me toward the mattress. We flopped onto the bed, never breaking the kiss, and I groaned into his mouth as our hard shafts rubbed, precum smearing between our heated skin.

"I get to pick the position," Nix whispered.

Without even the slightest hesitation—because I trusted Nix and wanted to experience everything with him—I reached down a gripped his ass. "You do. What's your pick?" I had a bit of apprehension surrounding both topping and bottoming—but I also knew Nix wouldn't force me into any situation I wasn't comfortable with.

"My pick," he said between pecking kisses all over my face,

"is…" Nix popped up on his elbows and gazed down at me with such love and devotion in his eyes—I'd never felt so cherished, so desired, so special to someone. "My pick is to let you decide. I'm so damn down with anything and everything, I'm letting you pick. Blow jobs? Hand jobs? Rimming? Fingers? Dildos? Top? Bottom? Yes, my answer is yes."

"You want *all* of that?" I teased. "Might be a bit much for one night."

Nix leaned in to bite my earlobe. "That's why it works out perfectly we have the rest of our lives."

We kissed for several long, slow moments, our cocks rutting together as our hands, lips, and tongues explored.

Weighing the desire I had to do *more* than what we'd done —although, I knew I'd be perfectly happy with our sex life for the rest of forever even if penetration ended up being something we didn't really want—with my nerves over bottoming and Nix's earlier words about always being assumed to be a top, I made my decision. "I wanna be inside you," I whispered. "This first time. I'm not against taking you next time, but I want to fuck you," I murmured against his lips.

Nix groaned and his dick twitched against mine. Then he froze. "Shit. Do you have lube? Do we need condoms?" He bit his lip. "Don't tell Otto I just insinuated we might have sex without protection—it's like having a teen at home, *do as I say, not as I do.*"

I laughed. "I have lube. Just because I'm demi doesn't mean I don't get myself off—I definitely do."

Nix moaned. "One of these days, I'm going to ask to see that."

"Condoms? I've never had sex with another person. What's your status?"

"I'm negative. I get tested yearly, more often if I've been

sexually active." Nix took my chin in hand. "If you're comfortable with it, I wanna feel you bare."

"I am." I leaned in and kissed him. "Apologies ahead of time if this isn't the best and it's over way too quick."

He shook his head. "Not possible. Just having you pressed against me is better than anything I've ever had. Knowing you want to fuck me already has me almost blowing my load. If you get off before me, I'm pretty sure we can work something out." Nix winked and I immediately imagined coming inside him and then watching as he jacked off and shot all over my face.

"Let me suck you," I said, shifting under him so I could shimmy down the mattress and take his thick cock between my lips. I hummed around his shaft as Nix grunted.

"Damn, now who's not going to last," he mumbled. "Fuck, for real, Charlie. You can't do that for too long."

I savored the slick heat of his cock sliding between my lips for a few moments before Nix pulled out and rolled me to my stomach.

"My turn to drive you crazy," he growled, hitching up my hips and spreading my ass. A quick flick of his tongue against my hole had me whimpering as I dropped my face to the mattress. "This okay?"

"God, yeah," I said, my words muffled.

Nix swirled his tongue around my entrance while cupping my balls and stroking my cock. "Can't wait to watch this pretty ass take me," he whispered, his hot breath tickling my sensitive skin.

I could have come right there with only a few more licks and strokes, but I wanted more. "Stop, it's too much. I need to be inside you." Rolling to the side, I fumbled in the drawer for lube. "How do you want to be?"

Nix flopped onto his back and spread his legs. "Just like this. There's something sexy about the thought of you bending me over the bed and taking me from behind, but I want to watch as you sink that gorgeous cock into my ass."

With trembling hands, I slicked my cock, moaning as the contact pushed me closer and closer to the end. With a lubed finger, I teased Nix's pucker, working the digit in slowly like I always did with my own ass.

"Fuck," Nix grunted. "That's good. Do another."

"I don't want to go too fast," I said, not wanting to hurt him.

"You're not, it's so good. I like the stretch. Give me two."

I added a second finger, loving the way Nix's body opened for me.

"That's enough, fuck, Charlie. Need you inside." Nix spread his legs wider and fisted his thick cock.

Pulling my fingers from his heat, I gripped my dick and lined up my leaking cock head with his slick hole. The first press of my flared head into Nix's body had me groaning. Slowly, pressing bit-by-bit, I sank into his tight heat, loving the way his muscles tensed and relaxed as he adjusted to my shaft.

When my balls met with his ass, I paused and savored the tight, hot grip his body had on me. "You good?" I asked.

Nix, head back, eyes closed, pleasure painted on his gorgeous face, nodded. "Need you to move."

I shifted to lean on my hands, hovering over him, as I thrust my hips slowly. My balls were already tight, a light tingle building at the base of my spine.

"Get down here and kiss me while you fuck me," Nix demanded.

"Why am I not surprised you're a bossy bottom. Who knew when I finally found a guy to love he'd end up topping from the bottom," I teased, bending my arms to wrap under his shoulders and capturing his mouth with mine for a long, slow kiss.

"Best of both worlds," Nix murmured against my lips. "You feel so damn good. Never been like this."

Increasing my speed, I fucked into him harder and faster, loving the grunts and groans he made when I hit that spot deep inside. The sound of flesh slapping flesh and breathless panting filled the room. "Do you wanna come this way?"

"No, wanna feel you in me and then jerk off on your face," Nix said, his words gruff.

"God, yes." I ground my hips into him, loving the noises he made. With a final thrust, my body tensed and my cock pulsed deep in Nix's ass as I groaned his name.

Nix gripped his cock while I came in his ass. When I pulled from his body with a soft grunt, he rolled me to my back and knelt beside me, jerking his dick with his eyes glued to mine.

"Come for me," I moaned, reaching between his legs to fondle his tight balls.

Nix stroked himself hard and fast before a low growl escaped him and he gripped the headboard. "Open your mouth," he ordered.

Opening my mouth while I teased his balls, I waited until the first spurt of his release exploded on my face, licking the corner of my lips where a drop had landed. Nix grunted and groaned over me, rope after rope splattering onto my skin, my lips, my greedy tongue.

With a final gentle tug on his spent cock, Nix released himself and took me in his arms, showering me with kisses as he licked his release from my face and delved deep in my mouth with his warm, slick tongue.

We kissed for several long, languorous moments until we broke apart and lay together in a heap of breathlessness.

"We need to clean up," I said with a chuckle.

"What? Nah. I'm good," Nix teased.

"You've got my cum in your ass and I've got your cum on

my face, we're showering." I rolled from bed and pulled him with me. "Come on. If we sleep now, maybe we can go another round before morning."

Nix appeared to be totally on board with that idea as he yanked me toward the bathroom. "That changes everything. Let's get cleaned up."

TEN

NIX

I WOKE several hours later with Charlie in my arms, his ass curved into my big spoon and his hand holding mine against his chest. Having Charlie in my arms was something I'd quickly become addicted to and I never wanted to lose what we had.

How in the world did you become so attached so quickly?

It was something I'd thought about a lot.

I'd been curious and interested from day one, but had quickly morphed into thinking about forever. I hadn't moved to Briarton looking for love, but it seemed to have found me and I wasn't even mad.

Charlie was my person, my anchor, my soul mate.

The fact that he'd struggled his whole life to make connections and build friendships—relationships of any sort —yet he let *me* in was mind-boggling to say the least. At times, a wave of sadness would wash over me when I thought of how much time Charlie and I suffered in our past when we could have been building memories together. But then I'd realize it was very likely we both needed our past experiences to help us navigate and appreciate what we were building together.

While fate's timing may not have been *my* choice, I couldn't help but think she'd gotten everything just right.

"What time is it?" Charlie mumbled, rocking his ass into me.

"Very late or very early depending on how you look at it," I said, brushing a kiss against his ear. "Go back to sleep."

"What if I don't want to?"

I'd enjoyed watching Charlie come out of his shell around me—his confidence had grown and I loved that I was there to share it with him.

"Got something in mind?" I whispered, my words soft and gruff.

"I wanna feel you inside me," Charlie said as he pressed his ass against me. "Please."

I gripped his chin and turned his face toward mine, capturing his lips in a blistering kiss. "I'm not going to push you, but I won't deny you. We can do whatever you want and stop if *anything* isn't comfortable."

"Grab the lube. Want me to get the dildo?"

I groaned. "As hot as that sounds, no. I want to be the one getting you ready." I rolled slightly and grabbed the bottle of lubrication. "But keep that in mind for another time." Coming back to Charlie, I nudged him a bit, pressing his chest more flush with the mattress and bending his top leg a little.

Trailing kisses down his back, loving the way he sighed and shivered as I licked over a freckle on his lower back, I reached his ass. Moving his leg just slightly opened him up to my mouth and I delved my tongue between his ass cheeks, swirling the tip against his tight hole.

Charlie groaned and pressed his ass toward me. "God, that's so good."

As he writhed and whimpered under me, I tongue fucked his pucker until he was sloppy wet and pliant for me. Smearing lube on my fingers, I pressed one into him and hummed with satisfaction as his body opened easily for me. "Fuck, love seeing you take my finger."

"More. Give me two," Charlie begged.

I added my second finger and had to grip my cock to keep from coming when Charlie cried out, his tight muscle giving way for me.

"Nix, please," he panted. "I'm ready."

Wishing I had more self-control, but knowing I'd blow my load within minutes if Charlie kept up his sexy begging, I slipped my fingers from his ass and lubed my leaking cock. "This position okay for you?"

"I'll tell you if it's not," Charlie said, his voice strained as he hiked his bent leg higher, opening himself wide for me.

"You're so damn gorgeous," I muttered, gripping the base of my cock and pressing it against his well-worked hole. I damn near lost my mind as I inched my way into Charlie's tight, hot body. "Fuck," I grunted.

"So damn good," Charlie whined, his voice muffled in the mattress. "God, Nix, it's so good." When I bottomed out, he gasped with a light chuckle. "Fucking hell, you're huge."

"You good?" I asked, gritting my teeth as I fought the urge to thrust into him.

"Yeah, so good. You can move."

Propped up on my arms, I started a slow pumping of my hips, watching Charlie's body take my long strokes as he whimpered. Everything about being with Charlie was night and day different than any guy in my past. Charlie was kisses and talking and hand holding *in addition* to fabulous sex—he wasn't the type to take something like what we were doing for granted or toss it away.

When he reached for my hand and gripped tightly,

moaning on a particularly hard and deep thrust, I dropped to my elbows and wrapped one arm under his chest while caressing the other down his torso. Reaching his half-hard cock, I gripped his shaft and stroked, smiling into his neck when he hissed. "This okay? Can you come?"

His answering grunt and thrust into my fist was enough for me. I increased the speed of my hips and jacked his now-rock-solid cock. When his ass clenched around me and a ragged sob escaped him, I slowed my thrusts but kept going deep as I leaned close and whispered, "You're so fucking tight and hot. Doing such a damn good job." Sucking his earlobe into my mouth, I fucked into him and ground my hips. "Love you, so damn much."

Charlie gripped my hand and moaned as his cock throbbed in my hand, shooting his release over my knuckles as his ass constricted around my dick. "Oh fuck, fuck, fuck," he cried as he came.

Watching Charlie come undone under me, *because* of me, drove me over the edge and I erupted with a low rumble as my cock spilled into him.

"Holy fuck," Charlie whispered, his words ragged and muffled as our sweat-slick skin pressed together, chests heaving as we caught our breaths. "Is it always that good?"

"Never has been before," I murmured. "I think we're just too damn perfect together."

"We're going to need to adjust our schedules."

I chuckled. "Why's that?"

"Gotta make room to fit *that* in at least once. Every day." He whimpered as my spent cock slipped from his ass.

"I'm not gonna argue." I rolled him to face me and grabbed a towel from the floor. Wiping us as clean as I could for the time being, I tossed the towel over my shoulder. "We'll shower in the morning. Sleep."

"Thank you," Charlie whispered. "For giving me that. For loving me. Just for being you. I love you."

"Love you." I pressed a kiss to his head.

"Their place is great," Charlie said as we rounded the corner of the sidewalk that lead to Morgan's house on the edge of town.

We'd walked over—partly because it was an amazing summer evening with an *almost* cool breeze keeping everything extremely pleasant, partly because Charlie had been writing all day and said he needed a walk to clear his head.

Morgan's home, from what he'd told me over coffee one day, had originally been a garage of some sort. The seller had renovated it to be one large apartment. The location was great because he was walking distance to Piping Hot—although, to be fair, almost everything in Briarton was pretty much *walking distance*. He had covered parking for his Jeep and a separate vehicle if needed, but I didn't think Justin had a car.

One of the best things about his location was he had no immediate neighbors and a huge backyard with a garden, a deck, and a hot tub.

"It is," I said. "I love my house and location, but being here with no neighbors would be nice sometimes."

Charlie pretended to be offended. "Hey, at least one of your neighbors isn't too bad." He bumped his hip against mine.

"I don't *mind* neighbors, and I love my yard, but I like the quiet stillness out here." Morgan's place was right at the edge of town where if you went farther out, you'd end up on farm land. Several farming families lived well-outside of Briarton's city limits.

"Even having neighbors, my place is so much quieter than the city, sometimes it's almost too quiet," Charlie said. "That's why I have to turn on white noise of some sort a lot of times if I'm going to be writing. Total silence almost always drowns out my words." He glanced around. "But it *is* nice and peaceful out here."

We headed to the backdoor as Justin had instructed.

"Love the hot tub," I gestured. "I really do think I want to put one in at my place."

"Would be a nice way to relax." Charlie took a deep breath.

"You okay?" I knew he'd brought up the idea of dinner with Justin and Morgan, but I wasn't sure he was completely comfortable with us going to their house rather than them coming to Charlie's.

"Yeah, I'm good. I like them, they're good people and I get along with them. Just my usual anxiety." He let go of my hand and rubbed his palms down his jeans.

I wrapped an arm around his waist. "Would it help if I told you how incredibly sexy you look and how I can't wait to get you out of those jeans later?"

Charlie sighed and smiled. "Maybe slightly." He kissed me. "I'm good."

I knocked at the door and a smiling Justin swung it open. "Hey! Come on in. Dinner is in the oven, but we've got wine."

Morgan met us in the kitchen. "Forgive Justin, he's excited to have company." He waved toward the rest of the apartment. "It's not huge, but I'll give you the grand tour before we sit down."

Inside, the apartment was bright and airy thanks to large windows. The exposed gray brick, black and gray pipes, black hardwood floors, and black wrought-iron shelving and dividers could have been cold and harsh, but Justin and Morgan had added their own touch of warmth with plants, candles, pillows, rugs, and books.

"So, it's very open-concept," Morgan explained.

I'd noticed the openness upon entering the front door. The kitchen was to the left with a small half-bath to the right next to a coat closet. Through the kitchen were the dining and living rooms. The living room flowed into a little office nook. The bedroom and main bath area were open to the apartment, but like other sections of the space were divided by large wrought-iron structures. A person at the front door could see all the way into the main bedroom, but the dividers gave a sense of separate rooms—almost like large, open screens between each section.

"Took me a while to get used to it when I moved in," Justin explained. "But I love it now."

"Yeah, I can see needing to adjust to basically having no walls," I said.

Morgan led us to the dining room and gestured for everyone to sit while he got the wine.

"Thanks for having us," Charlie said. I was probably the only one who recognized the slight nervous quiver in his words. "We'll have to return the favor soon."

"We'd love to come over sometime," Justin said.

With a few sips of wine and easy conversation, Charlie's anxiety appeared to ease.

"So, this is probably too forward," Justin said through a grin over his wine glass.

Morgan snorted and placed a hand on his husband's knee. "When has that ever stopped you?"

Justin shrugged. "Truth." His eyes sparkled. "Are you two doing the friends thing? Just hanging out since you're neighbors? Or..." he trailed off, brows raised.

Charlie cleared his throat, his cheeks pink. "Um, we're dating," he said just as I took his hand.

Justin did a little fist pump. "I knew it." He poured himself more wine. "At first, I thought you were just really hitting it off as friends, but the more I saw you two together, the more I was *sure* there was something more going on."

"Did you have a bet on us or something?" I asked.

Morgan chuckled. "No. He tried, but too many people have seen the way you two are around each other to bet against him."

Justin smiled warmly. "I just love this little town and all the love stories. Jo and Harley, Morgan and me, now you two." He sighed and sipped his wine.

"Who knew I'd move from a city of nearly nine hundred thousand only to find my perfect match in a tiny little town like Briarton?" Charlie squeezed my hand.

"I get it," Morgan said. "When I came here, all I wanted was some quiet and the chance to get my head and heart back in working order." He put his arm around Justin. "But I found so much more than that."

"I just love your story," I said, the exquisite wine warming my blood and slowing my words just slightly. "I think I would have loved to be here to watch it all unfold."

Justin brushed a kiss over his husband's cheek. "It was kinda a mess for a while, but it all worked out in the end." He turned toward Charlie. "So, you're really buying Wayne's?"

Charlie nodded. "That's the plan. I spoke to the bank and met with Wayne. He's getting the papers drawn up. I'll have a lawyer take a look at them and if everything's okay, Wayne's will be mine." He'd been nervous for his meeting with Wayne, but it had gone smoothly.

I could hear the anxious anticipation in his words. He was

trying not to get too excited about the venture, but I knew he was eager to make it happen.

"That's so amazing," Justin said. "We'll be friends *and* business owners together. I came here to get away. At the time, I had my dream of opening a place like Piping Hot, but I figured it would be further down the line. When I found out the place was for sale, I couldn't believe my good luck."

"It's not one hundred percent done yet, but I'm excited." Charlie finished his wine. "That's why I brought up this dinner. I was hoping we could talk business for a bit. I have some additions I want to bring to Wayne's, but I don't want to step on toes."

Justin rubbed his hands together. "Ohhh, I love a good brainstorming sesh."

A timer rang.

Morgan hopped up. "Let's eat first and then we can talk shop."

We spent at least an hour laughing and talking over an amazing lasagna, cheese bread, and salad. When Charlie and I insisted on helping with the dishes, Justin finally relented as long as we promised to be his guinea pigs for a new cookie he'd baked.

"I'm always up for trying baked goods of any sort," I said.

Justin grabbed two notebooks and tossed one to Charlie. "Okay, let's have it. What are your ideas?"

Charlie bit his lip, holding back a smile, and I could almost see the wheels in his brain turning. "So, I know you have a wine corner. I wanted to have that in Wayne's, but I was wondering about maybe doing a wine of the week. Like you do one and I'll do one and customers can vote for their favorites through ballot and purchases? I think it would be good for our shops to get people in *and* it would be good for the wineries."

Justin's eyes grew wide and he smiled. "I fucking love that idea." He scribbled in his notebook.

"Do you let the wineries rent a space or do you charge a percentage of each sale?" Charlie asked, making his own notes.

"We let them rent space for fifty a month and take five percent of each bottle sold," Justin explained. "The wine isn't a money maker for us, not really, but it allows us to do business with locals *and* brings in people who need a bottle of wine but don't want to drive to the winery. They often end up buying a coffee or treat while they're in the shop."

"I like that idea. So, let's work with the wineries and see what they think about a friendly competition."

Justin nodded. "Are you thinking one winery a week and we pit two of their wines against each other? Or put two separate wineries head-to-head?"

Charlie tapped his pen against his lip and I threw an amused smile Morgan's way. It was clear we both loved watching our guys in creative mode.

"I think either way has benefits, but I'm leaning more toward two wineries competing against each other. Winner gets to be named for the week or something like that."

"Works for me. I'll set up meetings within a couple weeks so you can settle in and then we can talk to the wineries." He made a note and then tapped his pen on his paper. "What else you got?"

"Have you guys thought about local honey?"

"Yes!" Justin crowed. "Morgan and I were just talking about that the other day. I think we have one farm in Briarton with hives, but I know there are several in the surrounding area. We want to get a nice display set up and have different apiaries represented through their different types of honey."

"Yeah, that sounds like what I was wanting to do. Do you

feel that we'd hurt each other in any way if we both sold local honey?" Charlie frowned.

"Not at all. I think the more we can sell local and the more we can just get people through our doors, the better."

"What about eggs? I didn't think a coffee shop would be interested in selling fresh eggs, but I wanted to be sure before I asked for locals to provide eggs at Wayne's." Charlie doodled a bit on his notebook.

"I think a lot of people would love buying fresh eggs, but it's not something we're doing at our place. Go for it," Justin said. "Maybe ask farmers about cheese? I don't know for sure if any of the surrounding farms make their own, but it couldn't hurt to ask. The great thing about Briarton is we're smack in the middle of several farming areas—there's a wealth of resources."

Charlie nodded. "I agree. Kinda wonder why Wayne didn't pull in more of the local items."

Justin shrugged. "I'm not sure his mind and heart have been completely into the shop the last few years. I think he probably hit a happy spot and didn't want to spend the time adding to it. He's been ready to move to Florida for a long time, I think he just felt obligated to stay here." He smiled. "But now that he's got a solid buyer who will keep Wayne's the same or better, he's good to go."

Charlie nodded and I saw the pride on his face—he was going to be crushed if something fell through with the purchase. "Okay, I know you guys let the craft and game shops set up displays, but you don't actually sell their items, right?"

"Right. They're here in town, so we display their items as examples, but people go to them to purchase." Justin leaned into Morgan's arm and whispered. "Can you start coffee?"

Morgan kissed him and headed to the kitchen while I continued to watch Justin and Charlie brainstorm.

"Well, I was wanting to have a sale display of local yarn. I need to chat with the craft store to see who they get their local yarn from. Maybe we can share." Charlie made a note. "Candles and soaps are my other idea for now."

Justin nodded. "I think local candles and soaps are an amazing idea. We steer clear of them at the shop because we try to keep our scents coming from the coffee, tea, treats, and food. We don't want to mix in soaps and candles—kinda overwhelming."

Charlie nodded. "Thoughts on me doing it at Wayne's? The way the place is laid out, there's the fresh produce, dairy, bakery, and meats section, but the soaps and candles could be in the grocery section with the other toiletries and such."

"Yeah, I think it's great. Definitely do it. I'm sure there are a lot of locals who would love to get their goods in your shop."

Charlie grimaced. "Not my shop yet." He wrote something. "Oh, I didn't want to assume, but I can still stock your coffees and teas, right?"

"Of course, I'd hoped you would. And we still plan to use you for our meats, breads, and most ingredients if that's okay?"

"Definitely." Charlie made another note and then paused to look at Justin before tearing out the notebook page.

Justin laughed. "Go for it."

Charlie folded his page of notes and tucked it in his pocket.

We moved to the living room for coffee and Justin's newest cookie concoction which turned out to be a delicious peaches and cream treat. I could have eaten an entire batch.

As we enjoyed cookies and coffee, Morgan stretched.

"You guys wanna use the hot tub? We've got plenty of extra trunks." Justin waggled his brows. "I'd say you could go without, but this isn't the start of a really cheesy porn."

We all laughed. I glanced at Charlie and he shrugged. That was answer enough for me.

Morgan pulled out five choices in trunks and pointed us toward the half-bath since it had a door.

As Charlie and I stripped out of our clothes, folding everything and neatly stacking our piles on the sink rather than strewing them all over like we might have done at home, I couldn't help but laugh at two grown men stuffed in a bathroom getting naked and putting on borrowed swim trunks.

Charlie joined me in the laughing, wrapping his arms around me and kissing me. The light and easy kiss soon morphed into something hot and deep, but Charlie jerked away.

"Oh my God, I'm not wearing someone else's trunks with a raging boner," he whispered and shoved at my chest. "Control yourself," he teased.

A few moments later, at least three of the four of us sighed as we sank into the warm, bubbly water.

"Dang, is that what I have to look forward to when I'm old? Aches and pains and groaning as I sit down?" Justin teased.

Charlie and I stared at him in awe as Morgan rolled his eyes.

"Excuse him, his immaturity and youth are showing."

Charlie glanced at me and gave me a look. In unison, we both splashed water toward Justin and he yelped.

Morgan, Charlie, and I laughed.

Justin groused as he wiped water from his face.

"Just for that, I should let you know that Morgan and I have sex in this every night and we don't clean it. You're basically boiling in a steaming cauldron of our sweat, skin, and cum."

"Oh my God, shut up," Morgan said as he yanked Justin

close with an arm wrapped around his neck and knuckles messing the younger man's already wet hair. "He's lying, obviously. The chemicals keep it clean and I wash it regularly."

"Notice he didn't deny the sex," Justin teased.

Not gonna lie, the thought of sex with Charlie in a hot tub had me moving ahead my plans to install one.

"The first time we sat in this, Morgan told me that Jo and my grandpa sometimes came to visit. I freaked myself out thinking I was sitting in a soup of their juices."

Charlie snorted. "That's gross and highly imaginative."

Justin smiled proudly. "Thanks. Morgan just told me I clearly didn't know how chemicals work. But whatever."

Morgan produced another bottle of wine and glasses I hadn't even known he'd brought outside. We all sipped fantastic wine and enjoyed the bubbly, steamy water.

"Oh my God," Justin exclaimed. "You know what people are going to think?"

The three of us eyed him warily. I'd learned quickly that you couldn't always be sure what Justin was going to say.

"They're going to think we're all sleeping together." He held up a hand. "Don't get me wrong, I'm not one to judge. Poly couples exist and they are valid. I'm just not a sharer." He hooked an arm around Morgan's neck. "But I guarantee there are people around here who automatically assume that gay couples are promiscuous and can't keep it in our pants; they'll have us pegged as a quad before the end of the week." He cackled. "Again, I'm not against others doing it— although, I think quads are fairly rare. A triad or throuple would be difficult enough, I think. It's just kinda funny—like in an annoying way—that so many people think of gay men just by who we're sleeping with. Like, Morgan and I have amazing sex, don't get me wrong."

I could feel the heat of Charlie's cheeks next to me and I

wondered if he was thinking about *our* amazing sex. I knew I was.

"But we're so much more than just our sex lives. We're successful business owners, I'm a bomb-ass baker, we've completed a marathon, Morgan has found success in real estate recently." Justin leaned into Morgan's arm. "I don't go around wondering about who Karen, Barb, Mitch, and Chad are sleeping with so why are people so concerned about who gay men are sleeping with?" Justin drained the rest of his wine and gave us a crooked smile. "Sorry, wine makes me talk a lot and I got agitated."

Morgan kissed the top of his head. "It makes him talk a lot until a certain point and then he just passes out."

We chatted a bit longer about the gossip mill in Briarton and finally decided to call it a night. As Charlie and I walked home, hand-in-hand, I couldn't help but smile. We'd had a great time with people I was happy to call friends, Charlie had been able to loosen up and enjoy the evening, and I'd gotten to watch him make plans for something he was excited about.

Life was good.

Three weeks later, life was still good, but a hiccup made some waves.

Charlie was now the proud owner of Wayne's and he'd been welcomed with open arms. He'd adjusted his writing schedule to account for him being at the shop at least a couple hours a day—or out meeting with local farmers and artists about selling their items—and he hadn't missed a beat.

I worried at times. He was still pounding out the words and had edits coming back soon, but he was also adding in a lot of new work at the store. So far, Charlie was keeping up, but I had concerns—even the best of them crash.

In all honesty, I hoped he'd eventually let his highly competent workers mostly run the place and he could just reap the benefits. He wasn't the type to not have his hand in the store at least somewhat, but I wanted him to find a good balance.

Charlie had surprised us both with how much he enjoyed visiting with customers. Okay, maybe *enjoyed* wasn't the right word. He tolerated it and found something good with each encounter.

I think living in such a small town had given Charlie the chance to let down his guard and get to know people. While he missed the anonymity of a large city, Briarton folks were just plain ol' good and Charlie's writer brain had figured out how to engage and gather tidbits to fill his creative well.

We often spent evenings chatting and laughing about things customers had said to him during his time at the store.

"Seriously, the people around here are so great, I could probably piece together at least five whole characters just based on things said, personality traits, and stories I've been told in the last three weeks."

He'd implemented a couple of his new ideas—so far, the most popular one was the wine competition between Piping Hot and Wayne's. The locals were loving the fun and the wineries had indicated they'd had more traffic to their websites and customers coming to sample and buy wines.

My own work continued to be highly rewarding and I thought I'd likely found my last new location and new job. My patients were absolutely amazing and I loved each and every visit with them.

Doctor Pierce was in the process of hiring another home health nurse, but the new person would be working only part time in the beginning. One of the fun facts about Briarton and the surrounding area was a lot of singles and families had happily made it their home in the past few years, but the population also boasted a large number of elderly folks who were happy to have home health care available.

Charlie and I had fallen into a very easy, very enjoyable routine of nights and mornings together—in one bed or the other—and often found time in our schedules to grab lunch or coffee with three creams, three sugars, and one pump vanilla. Every minute with him was new and exciting, yet our entire relationship felt as warm and comfortable as a favorite sweater worn for years and years.

I wasn't completely sure how Charlie and I would work out our living arrangements and whatnot in the future, but I knew in the very deepest recesses of my heart Charlie was my person. He was it for me.

One of the great things about both of us being older when we met, Charlie and I both knew ourselves, knew what we wanted, and knew we weren't looking for just a fling. We'd both been shocked by the speed and intensity of our relationship, but it had been pretty easy to welcome it with open arms.

My mind was on Charlie as I walked through the front door after a day packed with home visits, funny patients, and a lot of paperwork. So. Much. Paperwork.

Knowing Charlie was coming over for dinner, I put some hamburger out to thaw, played with CoJack and Cheddar for a bit, and headed upstairs to shower. Later, when I heard a door slam, I immediately went on alert—Charlie wasn't a door slammer.

I yanked on sweats and rushed downstairs to find Charlie bent over the counter, head in hands. My heart kicked into triple time, but I took a deep breath hoping to be a calm spot for Charlie.

"What's wrong?" I asked, placing a hand on his back.

"I should have known this whole damn thing was too good to be true," Charlie mumbled.

This thing? Was he talking about us? The store? His latest rounds of edits? A new contract?

"Gotta tell me a bit more. I can't help without specifics."

Charlie scoffed. "Help. Good ol' Nix, always wanting to help." He stood and ran both hands over his face. "Ever think there are some things you just can't fix?"

He was angry and hurt, but his words jabbed at me. Charlie wasn't the type to look for a fight and he didn't have much experience with heated conversations anyway. If he was lashing out, I knew he was beyond upset—likely scared.

"Of course, but that doesn't mean I won't try. Even if it's just to listen, I'm here." I tipped Charlie's chin and met his distraught eyes.

His wall cracked and his face fell—letting me see all his pain and worry—as he buried his head in my neck. "I'm sorry. I'm being an ass. I shouldn't have slammed the door. I shouldn't have lashed out at you."

I held him for a long moment, my hands rubbing up and down his back. "You wanna talk about it?"

Charlie sighed. "I don't know if I can. I've been a mess all afternoon."

"Okay, so it's not an *us* issue?" I couldn't help my worry even though I *knew* things were solid between us.

Charlie looked at me, horrified. "What? No. What the hell? Of course, not." He cupped the side of my face and kissed me, pausing long enough to slip his tongue between my lips and make love to my mouth almost as if drawing strength from the connection. "I'm sorry, I didn't mean to worry you."

"Tell me what's going on," I whispered against the corner of his mouth. "You want a drink? Eat first? Take a bath?"

"Let's sit on the couch." Charlie led the way and collapsed onto the cushion, his face falling into his hands as the cats scattered.

I sat next to him, my anxiety increasing with each rapid heartbeat.

"I had an interesting customer today," Charlie began.

I waited and let him tell the story.

"Mr. Maxwell's grandson, Stephen—and let me tell you, he's an asshole, nothing at all like Wayne. Anyway, he waltzed in with his fancy suit and smug smirk and asked to speak to the *temporary owner*." Charlie huffed. "Damn it, it's like he knew immediately how to set me on edge. I sounded like a scared kid in the principal's office when I told him I was the owner. He shook my hand and leaned in to whisper *temporary*. He then proceeded to tell me he was contesting the sale of Wayne's and I had two options."

"Asshole," I mumbled. I hated the man for putting Charlie in an uncomfortable situation.

"He says I can fight him. Which of course will be costly and long and drawn out."

"Or?"

Charlie sighed. "Or, he'll buy me out and the whole thing will be done within a week or less. Told me I can go back to my quiet little life and not have to worry about anything."

My nails bit into my palms. "What did you tell him?"

Charlie groaned and threw up his hands, standing to pace the room. "What was I supposed to tell him? I don't have the time or money to devote to a legal battle." He whirled around, pain etched on his face. "But that place is *mine*. It's my dream, it's *my* baby now. I don't want to just roll over and give up."

"Then don't." I stood and faced him. "We'll fight it."

Charlie walked into my open arms. "I don't know. Maybe I'm not cut out for this. Owning that place was supposed to just be a fun little venture in addition to my writing. I'm not one to take on a legal battle. What would that even mean for the store while we fought with Stephen?" He melted into my embrace. "Maybe it's best that I just let him buy me out."

"I'll support whatever you decide, but I need you to listen to me." I pulled back and caught his eye. "That place is *yours*. You don't have to give it up. We've got friends with a lot of connections—I say you don't make a decision until we talk to a lawyer at least." When tears threatened to spill from Charlie's eyes, I continued. "The well-being of this town isn't your sole responsibility, but I need you to think about this Stephen guy. Does he seem like the type to keep a small-town grocery running for the benefit of the town?"

Charlie's eyes went wide. "Not at all. Oh God, what do you think he'll do with it?"

"From what I've heard from Harley and Jo, the grandson has been hell-bent on tearing the store down and building apartments."

His nostrils flared. "No way. I won't let that happen." But then his shoulders drooped. "How in the hell am I supposed to stop him?"

"Let's talk to Jo and Harley, see if Justin and Morgan have any ideas, pull in a lawyer to at least get legal advice. Don't give up just yet."

Charlie nodded and tucked his head into my neck. "I really am sorry for slamming doors and yelling."

"Apology accepted. Next time, contact me instead of stewing all afternoon. Now, you wanna talk some more? Fix dinner? Bath?"

He was interrupted in answering when his phone chimed. Charlie studied the screen and frowned. "It's Stephen. Wants to know my decision."

"Tell him you'll be meeting with your lawyers on Monday and they'll be in contact."

Charlie tapped out the message and then gave me a wan smile. "You're sexy when you get all tough and bossy."

"Mmhm," I hummed as I kissed his neck.

"Let's eat and then a bath. I'm exhausted."

We each made a phone call while the burgers cooked on the grill. Jo Ellen was furious and only Harley in the background telling her to wait until tomorrow kept her from rushing to my house. Morgan and Justin both agreed to meet with us the next day. Jo and Harley were each bringing a lawyer with them.

By the time we ate and did a quick clean up—thank goodness for paper and plastic—Charlie was dragging when I filled the bathtub.

Later, in the dark of my room, Charlie gave himself to me, begging for me to make him forget, to remind him of all the good in his life. As his body clung to mine and I promised to love him forever, I spilled into him while his body quaked and took everything I had to give.

ELEVEN

CHARLIE

I WOKE with a headache and a boulder on my chest.

Well, CoJack was on my chest, but even after I gave him some loving and shooed him away, the weight of everything from the day before was still a heavy presence.

Thank God for Nixon. I should have called him immediately after Stephen left, but I was so worked up—angry and scared—I didn't want to disturb his appointments with patients. It wasn't a life or death emergency and I was a grown man, I could handle a few hours of freaking out on my own.

But that didn't mean I wasn't grateful for Nix's support.

Shifting in Nix's bed, trying not to wake him, I closed my eyes and ran through what Stephen had said. I didn't want to give up the store. Had the asshole grandson shown up before the sale, I would have maybe thrown in the towel and told Wayne to sell to Stephen—or *whoever*—but to not involve me.

However, Wayne's was now *mine* and I wasn't willing to just let it go. Brainstorming with Justin had been too much fun. Getting to know my employees and seeing how everything ran like a well-oiled machine had piqued my curiosity and given my creativity a boost. Meeting customers had brought so many smiles to my face—yeah, I had to limit my socializing time or I'd deplete my reserves way too quickly, but I still liked chatting here and there with the folks who came into Wayne's.

I did *not* have it in me—money or emotional fortitude—to get into a long, drawn-out, expensive legal battle. *But* I also didn't have it in me to just roll over and give up. I wasn't sure how likely it was that I could fight Stephen and win, but I wasn't going down without at least a preliminary fight.

We were meeting with our friends and their lawyers—I'd even thought about calling my agent and seeing if she had suggestions for a lawyer I could contact—and then I'd go from there.

Maybe the meeting would prove to me I was better to just sell. Maybe I'd learn I had more than one leg to stand on. Either way, I wanted to see just what was what before I made a decision.

As my brain stirred and agitated the soup of jumbled thoughts, I contemplated just getting out of bed since it was evident I wasn't going back to sleep anytime soon. But a warm hand on my thigh sent my thoughts scurrying another direction and I smiled.

Nix caressed his warm hand over my leg before trailing fingers along my morning erection. "I can hear your brain chugging away," he mumbled. "Wanna get your mind off things for a little while?"

I groaned when his fingers wrapped around my cock. "I'd love to, but I'm a little too sore after last night."

Nix popped up on an elbow. "I'm sorry, I hurt you?"

Chuckling, I shook my head and enjoyed his gentle strokes on my shaft, loving the way he thumbed through the precum on my slit. "No, it was great. Just what I needed. But you're really big and I don't think I've recovered enough to do it again right now."

Nix leaned down to kiss me. "In that case, you wanna take your mind off things by letting your boyfriend ride you?"

My cock twitched in his hand. "I'm definitely on board with that."

Nix moved to suck my cock between his lips, slicking me with his hot mouth. When he cupped my balls and took me to the back of his throat, I moaned.

"You keep that up for too long and there won't be anything left to ride," I said.

Nix popped off my dick and smiled, kissing me before reaching for the lube. He straddled my waist and slicked himself and my cock before tossing the bottle to the side.

I wasn't a tiny guy, average height and weight, but there was just something about being with a bigger man that sent shivers through me. Nix was taller, broader, and bigger than me in every sense of the word. Having him above me, preparing to take me into his body, engulfing me with his size heated me from the inside out. My big teddy bear, my gentle giant—I loved that he was so willing to help me forget.

Nix lowered himself onto my rigid cock, his thick thighs squeezing my torso as he hissed with the stretch. When he bottomed out, Nix started to grind his ass on me. Sliding in and out of his tight heat was amazing, but having him grind and roll his hips on my cock was fucking fantastic.

He rode me for several long moments, eyes on mine, pleasure and love the only focus.

When he reached behind to fondle my balls and found them hot and tight, Nix took hold of the headboard. "Fuck me," he whispered, demanding and sure.

Bending my knees for leverage, I thrust hard and fast into Nix's ass, chasing my orgasm and a momentary reprieve from the heavy thoughts.

"Shit, Charlie," Nix cried out. "Give it to me, wanna feel you."

My cock exploded in Nix's ass and I sank into the euphoria washing over me.

Nix gripped his shaft and jerked himself until his release shot over my belly and chest. With a wince, he lifted himself and let my cock slip from his body before collapsing on top of me and gathering me into his warm embrace.

"Good morning," he whispered against my jaw before kissing a path down my neck.

"Good morning." I slapped his ass. "And thank you. That was a nice diversion."

"Glad to be of assistance." He checked the time. "We should get ready. I'm going to get two patients in before our meeting. You should try to write, even if it's just to get the shit out of your head."

"Yep," I agreed. "And I need coffee."

Our meeting was at Jo and Harley's place, so we'd likely stop by Piping Hot for drinks on our way. But I needed caffeine long before that.

"Showers, coffee, and breakfast." Nix rolled from the bed and held out his hand. "Come on."

An hour later, I kissed Nix and told the cats goodbye before heading to Otto's place for a check-in. I needed to fill him in on what was going on. Then I *had* to get to my office and do some work before the meeting.

If I was lucky, my brain would allow me to compartmentalize enough to do that.

Armed with our matching coffee drinks, Nix and I ascended Jo Ellen's front steps. We were met by a wet hen.

Okay, we were met by Jo, but she was the definition of an old, wet hen.

Angry.

"Let them in the door, dear," Harley said from her side. "Sorry, boys. She's been worked up since you called. Come in, come in. Jo has notes and plans and a lot of energy."

Grateful for the support, I followed Nix to the large dining room table. We were introduced to Jo's attorney, Charles Hanson, and Harley's attorney, Edward Kane. Morgan shook our hands and Justin gave us hugs.

"Okay, Charlie, start from the beginning for Charles and Edward," Jo Ellen said. "Oh, and everyone help yourself to coffee and cookies, thanks to Justin and Morgan being dears and bringing goodies."

"Well, a little over a month ago, I heard that Wayne's was going to be up for sale. I agreed to Harley and Jo putting in a good word for me and letting Wayne know I was interested. About a week later—I can be more specific with dates if you need them," I said, pausing to check with the lawyers.

They waved me off—not dismissively, but it unnerved me. Maybe they didn't need dates because there was nothing they could do.

"Anyway, Mr. Maxwell called me and quoted a price. Said he was hoping to make the sale quick and easy because he wanted to leave for Florida with his wife." I took a fortifying sip of my sweet, creamy coffee. "I checked with my bank—I have money from my father's death—and Wayne's attorney drew up the paperwork. I had Mr. Kane take a look to make sure all was legit and the sale was finalized." I'd been grateful to Harley for his suggestion I used Edward Kane—I needed someone I knew could be trusted and Kane had a stellar reputation.

Mr. Kane nodded. "The sale happened quickly, but the

paperwork was all in good order. The sale was legal and binding."

"So, yesterday—I've owned Wayne's for about three weeks—this guy shows up. Looks completely out of place in his suit. Asks to speak to the temporary owner." I pinch the bridge of my nose. "I'm not the most outgoing person and I despise confrontation of any type, so I was immediately on edge. I shook his hand, wanting to keep things friendly, and told him I was the owner."

Recalling the sneer on Stephen's face angered me and threatened to send me back into a tailspin. The way he'd made me feel so much less than him—inconsequential, like the dirt on the bottom of his shoe—roiled in my gut.

"He leaned close and whispered *temporary* as he shook my hand. Then he proceeded to tell me he was Wayne's grandson and he was contesting the sale of the *family* business. Told me my options were to fight him—and he'd make sure the legal proceedings were very long and very costly. Or I could let him buy me out—for a lot more money than I spent to purchase the store." My shoulders slumped. "And that brings us to the present."

Jo flattened her hand on the table. "I'll be damned if that man gets to buy the store and tear it down. That place is a staple in this community and I will *not* have him putting in an eye-sore apartment complex."

"What do we know about Stephen?" Mr. Hanson asked.

"Wayne was always disappointed with how ruthless and uncaring his youngest grandson turned out to be," Harley said. "The kid has been buying and tearing up small-town businesses left and right to hear Wayne tell it. He's got a lot going on in bigger cities, but seems to take the most pleasure in shaking up small towns. He was after Wayne for years to sell to him—offered him triple what Wayne ended up selling for. Stephen used to say one way or another he'd see the crappy little store—his words, not mine—torn down and something fancy put in its place."

Hanson and Kane both scribbled notes.

"Charlie, could we get copies of the sale papers?" Mr. Hanson asked.

I nodded and pulled out two neatly stapled packets of paper from the folder I'd brought with me.

"Excellent," Mr. Kane said.

"What's the best way to proceed here?" Jo Ellen asked.

Justin stuck his hand in the air. "I think we need to figure out what the options are, but also, what do *you* want to do, Charlie?"

Every head turned my direction and I was grateful for Nix's touch when he took my hand.

"I don't have extra money for a legal battle," I said. "I want to keep the store. One, because I like it and want to continue running it. Two, because I don't want to see it torn down and replaced with an apartment complex. Wayne's has been in this town for decades and I can't stand the thought of some big business coming in and messing up Briarton." I sighed and ran a hand through my hair. "But I can't devote a lot of emotional energy to fighting, even if I did have the money, which I don't."

Harley tapped his knuckles on the table. "Let's not worry about the time or money right now. I think we need to figure out what's going on on Stephen's end. Edward, you'd talked about reaching out to Wayne—talking to him from a professional standpoint rather than one of us reaching out to him as a friend—maybe get some more information regarding his grandson and particulars."

Edward leaned in. "Yes, I'd like to look into Stephen's background. See what I can dig up."

"And we'll scour these papers," Charles tapped at the packet, "I don't know if there's anything Stephen can actually *contest* about the sale. He may not have *liked* that Wayne sold to you, but I'm not sure there's anything he can do about it."

"We'll also be in contact with Stephen's attorney in regards to this unfortunate turn of events." Mr. Hanson slid the papers into his briefcase.

"What's our timeline here?" Jo asked.

"We'll have some information for you within a week—maybe not solid answers, but at least information. We can regroup then." Edward stood and shook hands with everyone. "Jo? Harley? Just so we're all clear, if Mr. Hillion doesn't have it in him, emotionally or financially, to fight this, will the two of you be requesting to do so in his stead?"

My head whipped toward the older couple.

Harley nodded. "If it comes to that, yes. Jo and I will do the fighting."

"I can't ask you to…" I started, but Jo Ellen held up a hand.

"Charlie, you're not asking. My late husband and I had a solid hand in building this town way back when and I've done my damnedest keeping it the way we envisioned it. Sure, we've had to adapt to changes and what the town needs, but a high-rise apartment complex in a tiny town like Briarton would be just the first step in our ruin. I won't let it happen." Jo placed a hand on my shoulder. "You're not asking. This isn't so much about you as it is about this town. I'd be doing this no matter what."

I swallowed thickly and nodded.

"We'll be in touch," Mr. Hanson said.

The attorneys left and the six of us sat in silence for several moments.

"So, what now?" Nix asked.

"Now, we go about our days as normal. See patients, run the coffee shop, keep Wayne's customers happy, write your words." Jo took another cookie from the plate. "I'd like to keep this on the downlow if possible. I don't think folks around here need to start fretting just yet."

Morgan placed his empty cup on the table. "I feel like there's more to this whole thing. Wayne clearly didn't want to sell to Stephen. Now Stephen is swooping in on an unsuspecting individual—I don't like it. Both because Charlie is a friend and because it stinks of something suspicious."

"Agreed. Let's let Hanson and Kane do their work and we'll see where things are in a week." Harley pushed his chair away from the table. "Now, if you'll excuse me, I have coffee and a walk with Otto. He's promised to tell me about his Woodstock experience."

"Oh Lord," I groaned. "I'm sure that will be *quite* the story."

The little group dispersed with promises to keep things as normal as possible.

The way my head was spinning, I wasn't sure that was going to be so easy.

Three days later, I was an absolute mess. I hadn't been able to write a word—okay, I'd written words, but they weren't worth reading.

My days were spent playing with Cricket and Hopper, pacing the house, taking my mind off things the best I could by visiting the shop, and worrying about shit I couldn't control. But even going to the shop caused me to worry—was I being ridiculous taking an interest when it soon wouldn't be mine? Would the townsfolk pick up on my stress and wonder what was going on?

My nights were spent wrapped in Nix's arms. He held me, let me talk, let me be quiet, and made love to me. He was the sole bright spot in the entire situation. Okay, that wasn't true. I had Otto and my friends. I had a stable income. I wouldn't be *ruined* if I lost the shop.

But Stephen was getting to me. He'd swooped in to take away something I'd always wanted. I'd barely had a taste of being a small-business owner and then *bam* he came along threatening to take it away.

All of a sudden, the sliver of confidence I'd slowly built through coming to Briarton, meeting Nix, falling in love, and making friends was shaken to the core. Maybe I didn't deserve all the good I'd found since moving here. Maybe I wasn't worth the trouble this whole thing with Wayne's was causing. Maybe I needed to just give up, go back to hiding in my office, and live out the rest of my life lonely and unhappy.

The thought of it made me cringe, but at least back when I was friendless and hidden away I wasn't having to deal with all the emotions I'd been slammed with recently.

Yeah, but think about the emotions of the past. Loneliness, doubt, feeling like you'd never be enough for someone to love. Do you want to go back to that?

I shook my head, my hand playing with the soft fur on top of Cricket's head.

Of course, I didn't want to go back to that. But I also hated the crippling worry I was experiencing over Wayne's. The feeling that everyone in town would have been better off if I'd never showed up.

Taking a deep breath, I ran a hand over my face. I knew the thoughts running through my head weren't true. I knew my anxiety had ramped up lately and I knew I needed to work to get into a different head space.

If I could write about it, get some physical exercise, clear my head, maybe I could get my head back in the game.

I forced myself to roll off the couch and grabbed my phone before heading over to Otto's place.

A slow stroll through the backyard was a nice little reprieve from the heaviness of my anxiety.

When I reached Otto's, he met me at the door.

"You look like shit," he groused.

"Thanks," I answered wryly. "Pretty much feel like it, too."

"No news from the Wayne fiasco?"

"Not yet."

"You've got every right to bow out, you know?" Otto shuffled into the living room and sat in his recliner.

"I know." I followed and sat on the edge of the couch. "I just want to see what's what before I make a decision." I scoffed at myself. "Which sounds pathetic. Like if it's not going to be too much time or money, I'll hang around, but if it's going to take too much out of me, I'll let two elderly people deal with it for me."

Otto waved me away. "You wanted to own the grocery, not deal with family and legal drama. No one would blame you if you opt out."

Flopping back against the couch, I sighed. "Part of me wants to. So badly. But then I remember all the times Dad insinuated I was a quitter or shouldn't even try for something I wanted because I wasn't good enough." I placed a hand on my chest as if rubbing away the old pain of the memory. "I don't want to give in. Not yet."

"Then keep fighting. You know you've got the whole town on your side."

I nodded, my eyes closed. "I think it's mainly just the unknown getting to me."

Otto sighed. "You wanna walk with me to get some coffee? I could use a macaron, too."

Knowing my uncle was just trying to distract me, I ran a hand over my face. "Not really, but yeah, let's go."

We enjoyed the nice weather on our walk—it was slightly

more humid than I liked, but still a nice day—and reached Piping Hot. The little shop was busy as usual and Otto and I made our way inside.

I heard the laugh before I saw him.

Spinning around, I found Nix.

Sitting with a very attractive, smiling man.

Immediately, I fought away dread. Which was absolutely ridiculous, but the apprehension filled me all the same.

Nix knew a lot of people. Just because this guy was hot and my boyfriend seemed to be greatly enjoying laughing with him, didn't mean anything.

Or it could mean that Nix deserves someone better than an introvert who doesn't even know how to make friends.

"I don't know where your head just went," Otto said from my side as he waved at Nix, "but your boyfriend is calling us over to his table. Let's get our coffee and go meet his *friend*. That man of yours is nothing if not honest and loyal, so get your head out of your ass."

I shook myself free of the doubt and worry the best I could and placed my order. Justin gave me a wink and said he'd bring it out.

I followed Otto to Nix's table.

Nix stood and kissed my cheek. "Hey, you get some words down?"

I shook my head and glanced toward the other man.

"Maybe later," Nix said. "Otto, Charlie, this is a friend I used to work with. Joshua, this is my boyfriend, Charlie, and his uncle, Otto."

Cutie Joshua stood and shook hands. "Nice to meet you both. Nix hasn't been able to stop talking about you guys and his great new town." He winked. "Almost makes me want to move here."

I gave a small smile. "I bet."

We all sat down. Nix put his hand on my knee, but I was

twitchy and the only thing running through my head was I needed to escape. Be by myself. Hide. Not have to deal with the anxiety.

"Nix was telling me about some of the bars nearby, thought we might hit some of them while I'm here. Relive a little of the past," Joshua said. "You in?"

Our order arrived, thank God I'd asked for it to go. "Um, I'll have to pass. I have a deadline to meet and some personal issues going on. You two enjoy." I grabbed my coffee and muffin and stood, turning to Otto. "I need to get back, you coming?"

He narrowed his eyes at me, but nodded.

Nix placed a hand on my hip. "You good?"

"Yeah, gotta work. Have fun."

"I'll see you after work?" Nix asked, concern etched on his face.

"Um, maybe. Deadline, ya know?" I needed to get out of that coffee shop before I had an anxiety attack.

"I'll text you," Nix said.

I gave a quick nod, feeling like a complete ass for being rude and weird. I rushed to the sidewalk, ignoring Morgan's greeting as I bolted.

I was nearly half a block away before I slowed slightly.

"Damn it, Charlie," Otto huffed behind me and I stopped in my tracks. No matter how upset I was, I couldn't make the old man run.

"Sorry." I shifted my coffee and muffin bag so I could take Otto's order from him. "Let me carry that."

"What the actual fuck was that?" my uncle demanded.

"I don't know," I said, not even trying to pretend like I didn't know what he was talking about. "I just needed to get out of there."

"Because your loving and devoted boyfriend was chatting with an old friend?" Otto elbowed me as we got closer to home. "That doesn't seem like you. You've never seemed to be the jealous type."

I shrugged, feeling sheepish. "I've also never had anyone to be jealous over."

Otto snorted. "You really think you have anything to worry about with Nix?"

"Cheating?" I ran the thought through my head. "No."

"Then what's up?"

"I don't know. I need to lock myself in my office and do some work." Shutting out the world—ignoring the worry and uncertainty and doubt washing over me the past several days —sounded like a great move.

"You *need* to reflect on what just happened and talk to Nix."

I helped Otto into his house and turned down his invitation to stay and chat. "Really just want to get home and be alone. Need some time to regroup."

"That's fine. Everyone needs that from time-to-time." Otto slapped me on the back before popping a macaron into his mouth. "Just don't stay hidden for too long. That's not fair to yourself or to Nix."

I frowned, thinking about my sweet, loving teddy bear.

"He's not going to understand what's going on if you don't talk to him." Otto walked with me to the door.

"I don't know that I even understand what's going on." I said goodbye and moped my way back home.

What the hell was going on with me? Jealousy didn't seem to be part of me, but I also wanted to punch Joshua in his young, cute, outgoing face. Sitting there being so full of laughter and easy chit-chat with *my* boyfriend. Talking about going out to clubs, socializing, having a great night out with *my* boyfriend.

Nix deserves someone like Joshua. He enjoys going out, having fun, meeting up with people and you can't give him that.

I flopped onto the couch and sipped my coffee. Cricket and Hopper came to comfort me and I fed them tiny bites of my muffin as I sank deeper and deeper into the thick heavy sludge of uncertainty and dread.

When I finished the muffin, I stood and walked to my office. I needed to write, but there was no way it was going to happen. I couldn't even form coherent thoughts let alone write words that made sense and entertained readers.

My entire body yearned for rest—my brain was mush and exhaustion blanketed me.

Frozen in the middle of my office for several moments, I attempted to make sense of my feelings. In the end, I walked to my bedroom and climbed into bed. The sheets smelled of Nix and my heart ached.

As I drifted off to sleep, my brain registered I wasn't afraid of losing Nix. I was scared to death of having to admit I wasn't the right guy for him and let him go.

By the time I woke, it was early evening and I had several missed messages from Nix and Otto. Even Stella had texted which told me Otto had contacted her.

I stared at the messages and felt frozen in indecision. I didn't want to have to think about what to say, what to do, *anything*. Dreading what I was going to read, I opened Nix's messages.

Nix: *Hey, you okay?*

    Nix: *I'm worried about you. You seemed off today.*

    Nix: *I'm hoping you're just locked up with your words and not ignoring me.*

    Nix: *Seriously, you're kinda freakin' me out.*

    Nix: *Charlie, answer me before I come over and knock down your door.*

Nix: *I have a late appointment. Like it or not, I'm coming over after.*

I sighed as tears stung my eyes. It wasn't fair to make Nix worry. Even though I had no idea what was going on in my fucked-up head, I owed it to him to at least let him know I was alive. I hit *reply* and thumbed out my message.

Me: *Sorry, was asleep. Not great company tonight. Talk tomorrow?*

I didn't *want* to talk, but maybe after a good night's sleep, I'd feel better and be more equipped to handle myself like an adult.

Nix: *Sorry, that doesn't work for me. I'll be over when I finish up with my last patient.*

I groaned and flopped back down on the pillow. Looked like I didn't get a day to feel better. Rolling myself from the bed, I woodenly made my way to the bathroom where I somehow managed to clean myself, brush my teeth, and make my hair somewhat presentable.

Reality slapped me in the face.

I groaned as understanding dawned on me. The nap had at least cleared my head enough to know what was going on. I didn't know why it took so damn long for me to recognize it.

So stupid.

My anxiety and depression had been well-controlled for

quite some time. I took a low dose medication and spoke fairly regularly to a therapist.

Medication.

Which I hadn't gotten around to refilling upon moving to Briarton and ran out of it a couple weeks ago. There was a half-filled spare bottle somewhere in the house, but I hadn't bothered looking for it.

Therapy.

I'd cut ties with my therapist before the move—with the promise of finding someone once I got settled.

Which I obviously hadn't done.

The anxiety and depression may have reared their ugly heads no matter what—thanks to my slacking—but add in the stress of everything—the new place, adjusting my writing, meeting Nix, the mess with Wayne's—and I was bound to be a mess.

Seeing Nix with Joshua was just icing on the cake to my little break down.

I didn't think Nix would cheat.

Ever.

And without all the other shit going on, I likely wouldn't have reacted to meeting Joshua the way I did.

But I was smack-dab in the middle of a perfect storm and each factor played its part superbly.

Before I could let the haze of depression distract me, I called Dr. Pierce—told him I needed to see him as soon as possible about getting a prescription *and* to get his referral to a therapist. I left my number and asked him to call me sooner rather than later.

Then I dug through a few boxes I'd yet to unpack and found the prescription bottle of pills I'd so ridiculously allowed myself to think I didn't need. I wasn't one to think medication was a life-long requirement, but I also wasn't one to judge—myself or others—if a person *did* need the support of medication for their mental and physical health.

I walked the pill bottle to the kitchen where I put it on the window sill behind the sink and took a dose with a long drink of water.

As much as I hated the idea of trying to explain my recent slow breakdown to Nix, I knew we'd both be better for it once it was done. I headed over to Otto's place to make sure he'd eaten dinner. I'd wait for Nix to get finished with work from my uncle's house. Then we could have a good chat.

Except, Nix didn't text at his normal quitting time.

Or even an hour after.

Or even *two* hours after.

I was officially worried.

Okay, *pissed* was a word my fucked-up head wanted me to focus on.

Did he decide to go out with Joshua anyway? Left you hanging in favor of the young, bubbly, extrovert? So much for being concerned.

"If you keep staring at his house, you'll bore holes in it. Just go over there." Otto waved a hand toward Nix's place.

"He's not home. The house is completely dark." I paced the tiny cottage, obsessively glancing toward the shadowy silhouette of Nix's house as the sun dipped behind the horizon.

"Call him?" Otto suggested.

I waved my phone in the air. "He's not answering."

Otto frowned. "I'm not trying to load you down in this, but you seem a bit more settled now than earlier. Surely you realize you need to pull your head from your ass and fix this, right? Don't give up just because he's not home *right now* or not answering *right now*."

I nodded. "I know. I'm not giving up." I ran my hand over my face. "I figured it out. Stopped taking my medication," I paused and held my hands up in defense when my uncle started to rant, "I know, I know. It wasn't on purpose. I was feeling really good and things were going great, I spaced it. When the one bottle ran out, I just never got around for searching for the second bottle."

Otto narrowed his eyes. "Therapy?"

I shook my head.

"Damn it, Charlie." Otto's cheeks were red. "Here we are in this great little town with these great people and you're spending all of your time making sure I stay healthy, but I can't even pick up on the fact you're not doing the same for yourself."

"It's not your fault."

"Maybe not, but I should have paid better attention. Damn it."

"I called the doctor and started the medication again. Those two things aren't the *only* reason I've been a mess." I stared at Nix's empty house.

"The Wayne's situation?"

I nodded. "Yeah, the mix of all of it hasn't been good. Throw all of my shit on top of my self-doubt and that cute little fucker Joshua and it made for a spectacular freak out."

"It's good you have your past experiences and work with your therapist to recognize what's been going on," Otto said.

"Yeah." I took a deep breath. "Just wish I had realized it a bit sooner rather than getting to this point."

"Well, you can't change that."

"What if it's too late?" I asked, staring at Nix's house.

"Too late? Too late for what?"

"What if Nix realized I was too much trouble? What if he opted to go out with Joshua and it opened his eyes to how boring I am?"

"That's a bunch of bullshit and you know it. That boy is as head-over-heels in love with you as you are with him."

Otto yawned. "I'm gonna hit the hay. You let me know when you hear from Nix."

I stuck around long enough for Otto to get settled in bed with a movie and then headed back to my place. For an hour, I fretted and nearly wore a path in the carpet of my bedroom as I paced and watched Nix's house, uselessly redialing his number from time-to-time.

Where the fuck is he?

Just as I was about to call Morgan and Justin and get their advice—hell, maybe they'd seen him or maybe they had a suggestion for where I could find him—my phone rang.

It wasn't Nix.

"Hello?" I answered, my voice catching.

"Hello, this is Briarton County Community Hospital calling for a Charlie Hillion," a curt but professional sounding voice said.

My heart plummeted. "This is Charlie."

"Mr. Hillion, we have a patient by the name of Nixon Riley. Are you able to come to the hospital?"

"Oh my God, is he okay?" I rushed downstairs, grabbing my keys and sending the cats scurrying.

"We'd prefer to fill you in when you've arrived, please, sir."

Fighting back the simultaneous urge to scream and puke, I jumped into my car. "I'll be there."

For the next fifteen minutes as I drove to the hospital on the opposite side of the county from my house, I imagined every single horrible outcome possible.

Somehow my legs carried me toward the emergency room doors and I took a deep breath, steeling myself for whatever I was walking into.

TWELVE

NIX

I WINCED AS THE NURSE, Blake, finished the stitches on my forehead.

"Sorry, I know that pinches." He finalized his work and positioned a bag of ice on my shoulder. "You should be glad stitches is all you ended up with. No concussion is a miracle when it comes to cows and heads."

I laughed weakly, my forehead and shoulder both throbbing. "I'll keep that in mind. For now, I'm just ready to get home."

He looked over the device on his lap. "It looks like we'll be sending you on your way pretty soon. Can we call someone for you?"

"Charlie." I glanced around for my phone. "Shit, where's my phone?"

"Everything that came in with you is in this bag." Blake plopped a plastic bag onto my lap.

I searched through the bag which held my wallet and some loose change.

No phone.

"Shit." Clearly, the night had done a number on my ability to express myself.

"Write his name down for me." Blake handed me a scrap of paper.

"Charlie Hillion. He lives in Briarton. If you can't get hold of him, try these people next." I wrote down Morgan Perry, Justin Wade, and Harley Wade. "They're all in Briarton. Call Piping Hot if you need to."

"Okay, I'll get busy with your paperwork and do what I can to find you a ride home." Blake dimmed the lights in the little exam room. "Try to rest. You're fine to sleep since you don't have a concussion."

I nodded and shifted the ice on my shoulder with a groan. Easing back into the wholly-inadequate pillows, I recalled what had led up to me landing in the emergency room.

Charlie had been acting weird when I'd seen him earlier—okay, he'd actually been weird for several days, but I'd chalked it up to taking over Wayne's and the shit going on with Stephen.

His reaction to Joshua had been...well, not unexpected per se, but concerning. I wasn't sure Joshua even noticed Charlie's behavior being *off*, but I'd known something was wrong the moment I saw him walk into Piping Hot.

The tension etched on his face, his shortness, and the way he'd been like a scared animal looking to escape, all of those screamed to me he was struggling. When he hadn't answered my texts, I'd been beyond worried. If I hadn't had a day packed with appointments, I would have dropped everything to go talk to him, even though part of me insisted Charlie clearly wanted to be alone.

Instead, I'd seen patient after patient through the afternoon and into the evening. My newest patient lived on one of the farms outside of Briarton. His name was Bart and he was more cantankerous than Otto and a lot less fun, to be honest. His daughter had informed me Bart planned to keep from seeing me by claiming he wasn't available during the daytime. So, with his daughter's support, I'd offered to come at six o'clock in the evening.

I couldn't help but laugh as I recalled the look of irritation on Bart's face when I'd shown up. I didn't think I'd be going to see him more than maybe once a month based on his needs and my first meeting with him, but he was *not* happy to see me on his farm.

The appointment had taken a lot longer than the double slot I'd allotted for it—Bart was a grump and a storyteller and he stalled better than any patient I'd ever dealt with.

I'd finally promised him he could "teach the city-slicker" if he'd just let me do my job. He'd agreed to the exam and let me talk about health points I needed him to adhere to for his own safety.

Told me in no uncertain terms he would *not* be following any suggestions I made, but at least he allowed me to share the information.

Like I said, *fun* man.

When we'd finally finished, Bart had led me to the barn and told me to put down my bag. He'd pointed to a cow and grinned, somewhat evilly. "You ever milk a cow?"

I'd not been able to stop my eye roll and laugh. "Bart, do I *look* like a farm boy?"

He'd nodded and spat. "That's what I thought. Well, you're gonna learn. You come out here interrupting my life, you're gonna get something out of it."

"Well, I actually already get a lot out of treating my patients and making sure they're healthy, but I'm not gonna turn down the chance to learn this." I'd clapped my hands together. "Show me what to do."

Everything got a little fuzzy from that point on. Bart told

me I was setting his cows on edge, but when I offered to take a rain check, he'd balked.

"No way, no how. If you think you're coming out here again, you're gonna do something useful while you're here." He'd put a stool by the cow and told me to sit down.

Somewhere between me sitting on the stool and the point when I'd have done any actual *milking*, the cow spooked, I got knocked over, and two separate hooves found their way to land squarely against my shoulder and my forehead.

As head wounds go, the gash on my forehead bled as one would expect. That is to say it gushed. My shoulder hurt badly enough it *should* have been bleeding, but instead, it was just going to bruise spectacularly.

For his part, Bart felt bad and insisted his daughter drive me to the hospital—not that I would have been in any shape to drive even if I hadn't caught a ride with Harley and Jo on their way out of town earlier in the evening.

So, that was how I'd ended up in the emergency room with seven stitches in my head and a shoulder that felt as if it had been beaten with a baseball bat—or at least kicked by a cow.

I snorted at my sorry condition, grateful for the fact I didn't have a concussion, and wondered just where the hell my phone was. Likely on the damn barn floor, hopefully not smashed to pieces by a dairy cow.

The curtain surrounding my little cubicle moved and Blake smiled. "I think we may have found someone who is very anxious to see you."

A visibly shaken Charlie rushed around Blake as a sob escaped him. "Oh my God, they wouldn't tell me anything until I got here. You hadn't answered my calls and I had all of these horrible images of terrible things happening to you." He sat on the edge of my bed and took my hand. "Are you okay? What happened?"

Blake gave me a wink. "I'll be back with papers for you to sign."

"Went a couple rounds with a grumpy old farmer and won." I brushed my fingers over the throbbing gash in my head. "Went half a round with a sweet old cow and lost. Badly."

Charlie studied my head and then glanced at my shoulder. "Wait, what? A farmer did this?"

I chuckled and pulled away the ice pack. "No, his cow did this."

He gasped at my gnarly-looking shoulder. "What? How? Did it bite you? I thought cows were gentle."

"Well, I'm not exactly sure *what* spooked her—I truly don't think it was me—but in her freak out, she knocked me from the stool and then kicked me in the shoulder and head." I squeezed his hand. "I'm sorry for not calling or answering. I just realized I don't have my phone. I'm guessing it's in Bart's barn."

Charlie frowned. "There's so much to this story I'm not completely understanding. But you can tell me at home."

Home.

Honestly, just knowing Charlie came for me and referred to *home* was all I needed; I already felt better.

Blake showed up with paperwork for me to sign and Charlie grabbed my meager bag of belongings. Once reached the car, he tossed the bag in the back seat and grabbed my hand. Pulling me into a warm embrace, being careful of my shoulder, Charlie shuddered against me.

"I'm so sorry."

I kissed the top of his head. "My injuries have nothing to do with you. I don't have a concussion, the stitches will dissolve and hopefully leave a very rugged, sexy scar, and my shoulder has no tears, only a bruise."

Charlie nodded. "I want to hear more about this farm and cow, but I'm sorry for my actions today."

"Can we talk at home? I'm honestly about to drop."

We climbed into Charlie's car. He paused for a moment to check his phone. "Oh, Morgan says your medical bag and phone are at the shop." He looked at the time. "Want to run by and get them?"

"Can you just tell him I'll grab them tomorrow. And tell him thank you." Exhaustion crashed over me in waves. "I just want to get home, shower, and take you to bed."

Charlie shot me an incredulous look.

"Not *that*. At least, not tonight. But I have no restrictions since I'm not concussed. Just the pain of the stitches and the bruise." I yawned.

By the time we reached home, I'd filled Charlie in on Bart, the farm, and my first ever—and probably last—attempt at milking a cow. He parked in the garage and led me into his house.

"My place or yours?" he asked.

"Either is fine, but I need to feed my cats."

"Let me feed the boys and we'll go to your place," Charlie said as he made sure Cricket and Hopper had food and water. He frowned. "Unless you'd rather be on your own? It's okay if you need some space."

I shook my head. "Why would I need space? I need a shower and sleep, but I don't need to be alone."

Charlie took my hand and whispered, "Sometimes I need that."

"I know. And I did my best to respect that today. But it's hard when I don't know if you *need* space or something else is going on."

We walked through the moonlit path between his house and mine.

He nodded. "I know, I should have done a better job of explaining what I was feeling."

"I guess that's hard if you don't even completely understand it yourself." I wasn't *sure*, but I had a feeling Charlie had been pretty thrown off by whatever hit him so hard today.

Charlie huffed. "Yeah. I was definitely there."

We played with my cats for a few moments and left them to eat their very late dinner before heading upstairs.

"Give me ten minutes or less. Just wanna wash the grime away." I tossed the plastic hospital bag to the floor, my wallet thudding and the loose change clanking.

When I finished in the bathroom and joined Charlie in bed, both of us naked as if we *needed* the close connection, he sighed and snuggled close.

"You wanna tell me about it?" I asked, kissing the top of his head.

"You're tired, you want the short version?"

"No, I'm exhausted, but I don't think I can sleep just yet."

"Then I'll start at the beginning. Feel free to interrupt if needed." Charlie's fingers danced through my chest hair. "Moving here was probably the best thing that's ever happened to me. Which left me with a lot of guilt because the only way I got to move here was because my father died." He sighed. "I mean, I could have moved here no matter what, but the catalyst for Otto opting for Briarton was Orson dying.

"Even though moving here and meeting you was great, it was still stressful. Like not *distress*, but still a change and adjustment. Buying Wayne's was scary and a big step—one I felt ready for and comfortable with, but still another change and adjustment.

"I think at that point, I should have realized I needed to take a self-assessment of my mental health—just check in with myself. It's something my therapist used to encourage."

Charlie paused and met my eyes, a confusing look of guilt on his face. "Surprise, your boyfriend needs a therapist."

I gripped his chin. "Is there anything I've ever said or done to make you think I'd give one iota of a shit about you seeing a therapist? Anything to make it seem like I'm not a proponent of mental health?"

He shook his head. "No. Sorry, that's my fucked-up brain talking." He sighed. "Anyway, my spiral likely started long before Stephen. But him showing up, making me feel like scum on the bottom of his shoe, dredging up all of my doubt, and then the unknown and uncertainty of waiting to see what can be done in the situation increased the spiral." He paused and scowled. "Seeing you with Joshua—who is hella cute, by the way," Charlie grumped.

I laughed. "He *is*. And his new wife would probably agree."

Charlie buried his head in my chest. "Well, don't I feel even more like a total chump."

"Look, whether he was gay or straight, interested in me or not," I lifted Charlie's face to look at me, "I'm not the type to cheat or want more than what I've got. I had years to play the field and it wasn't a rewarding time in my life. Meeting you, falling in love, building a new life here, *those* things are the most rewarding moments I've ever lived through."

"When Otto forced me to think about it, I knew deep down you'd never cheat. It's just not who you are."

"Then what was going through that gorgeous head of yours?" I asked, truly wanting to know. Hoping I could help relieve whatever worries he had.

Charlie shivered. "It was on repeat. Joshua is cute. Joshua is young. Joshua loves socializing. Joshua loves going out. Joshua is all of these things you want and need and I'm none of them."

"You do know I don't *need* to go out and socialize, right?

Sure, I did that a lot in the past and I still enjoy it from time-to-time, but dinner with our friends, laughing with them over coffee, hanging out in the hot tub, that's a lot more my speed these days." I brushed a soft kiss over Charlie's lips, loving the way he melted into me. "Even if I still craved going out and meeting new people, it's not something I would expect you to do for me. I respect your comfort zone. I don't *want* to go out bar hopping, but if I did, I'd ask Justin or another friend to go along. And you'd know I was out having fun and completely trustworthy." I nuzzled my nose against his. "But honestly, the thought of bar hopping these days just makes me want to nap. I'd so much rather just drink wine and laugh with Justin and Morgan than even contemplate large crowds and all the hassle." Pressing my forehead against his, careful not to bump my stitches, I smiled. "People change. What I crave now is what I've found with you. I don't need the emptiness of what's in my past."

Charlie took a deep breath and hummed. "God, I love you so damn much. You're too amazing to be true. So, while we're being open and honest, I take medication for anxiety and depression. It's just a low dose…"

I interrupted him by clearing my throat and raising my brows.

Charlie blushed. "That sounds like an excuse, right?"

"Doesn't matter if it's the top-level dose, if you need it, you need it."

He nodded. "I know that and I'd tell anyone else that, it's just when it's about *me*, I feel like I constantly have to make excuses or validate things. Anyway, I take medication. When I moved here, I was almost out, but I had a few extra pills as an emergency stash until I could get settled. Well, I ran out and I was feeling so good, I didn't dig out the extra bottle."

I winced, knowing where he was going.

"So, yeah, stopped therapy, stopped meds, piled on a

bunch of changes and adjustments, *and* a really shitty, stressful situation." Charlie pursed his lips and breathed deeply. "Major breakdown."

Running my hand up and down his back, I kissed his temple. "All the ingredients for a perfect storm. I'm sorry you had to deal with that."

"I came home today—hell, is it still today?" He glanced toward the red-glowing alarm clock. "It was like I was in concrete, trying to function, but I couldn't move. The thought of doing anything gave me anxiety. The thought of ignoring everything gave me anxiety. Trying to move, trying to breathe, felt as if I was under a heavy, wet blanket. All I could do was sleep."

"Damn it, I'm so sorry, I wish I had been here."

"I don't think it would have helped."

"I could have at least held you. So, after your nap, you figured out what was going on?" My hand never stopped caressing Charlie's back.

He nodded. "Yeah, sleep gave me a brief moment of clarity and it all clicked into place. Way back before I started working with a therapist and taking medication, I would have floundered for a lot longer. But the skills I learned in therapy—even though I wasn't using them perfectly today— helped me realize it a lot quicker. And knowing what it feels like when my anxiety and depression are regulated made it easier to recognize when they aren't." Charlie worried his bottom lip. "I'm really sorry I never told you any of this before."

I shook my head. "You don't owe anyone an explanation. If talking about your mental health is helpful, do it. If it's not, you don't *have* to. It doesn't change how I feel about you now and it wouldn't have changed how I felt about you back when we first met."

"I started the medication I had left, and I called Dr. Pierce to get hooked up with a new therapist and get a new prescription."

"Those are good steps."

"I knew if I put it off, calling Dr. Pierce, I'd find excuses until things got even worse." Charlie yawned. "I really did know you'd never cheat on me. My head was just in such a state I truly believed you need someone better than me, someone like Joshua." He huffed. "And it's so crazy I can believe that because when I say it out loud—or when I do this thing I learned called putting my thoughts on trial—I *know* there's no truth in the thought. It's all in my head. But it's scary how easily I was able to believe the false narrative."

"Anxiety and depression don't speak the truth and they both know how to find your weaknesses and expose them. They don't play fair."

"I love you. Thank you for being here and for loving me through this." Charlie snuggled into me, our legs entwined.

"Nowhere I'd rather be." I kissed the top of his head. "I love you and we're a team. Whether we're taking on a cow hoof to the head, a bout of anxiety and depression, or an asshole grandson, we're in this together."

Charlie groaned. "Could we possibly be in it together for less stressful, happier things?" he asked with a chuckle.

"The good, the bad, sickness, and health," I whispered, and we both paused, eyes glued to each other. "And I mean that in every sense of the words. Maybe not *now*, but I don't need rings and a ceremony to make that pledge to you."

Charlie's eyes sparkled in the dim moonlight trickling through the window. "The good, the bad, sickness, and health," he repeated. "You're my person from here until eternity."

"And you're mine," I murmured against his lips.

He pressed close, sealing our promises with a hard kiss, then softening to deepen the contact. "I love you."

"I love you." I tucked Charlie into my chest and we fell asleep, exhausted from the day, the revelations, and the emotions of privately vowing to love each other through it all.

The next morning, I woke to my alarm—stiff and sore—and found my bed empty. Had Charlie gone home?

I showered, keeping the stitches dry and groaning as the warm water hit my bruise, before heading downstairs. Grateful I only had one appointment for the day—and I likely could reschedule if needed—I wanted coffee and time to recoup.

"Good morning," Charlie said with a bright smile as he came in the backdoor with a large bouquet of peonies.

"Good morning. How are things this morning?"

"I feel better. The anxiety and depression are still there, but recognizing them and talking about things helped me take back some control it felt as if I'd lost. I have the skills I've learned and those are helping. Definitely in a better state today than the last several and that's mainly because I finally put a name to what was going on, even if I didn't want to admit it."

I nod. "Sounds good. Don't worry if you slip or need help. I'm here."

"Thank you."

"You were up early."

"I went to feed the cats and check on Otto. I'll get words done later, hopefully—it's going to take a bit to get back on track, the medication doesn't work over night. Thought we could walk to get coffee and your stuff? Maybe see if Harley and Jo Ellen know anything from Hanson and Kane." He wrapped his free arm around my waist and kissed me. "These are for the patient. How are *you* feeling this morning?"

I kissed him back, long and slow. "All good, considering. My head doesn't ache—the stitches are sore. My shoulder hurts, but no more so than a football injury or a super painful vaccination."

"Why am I not surprised you played football?" Charlie handed me the flowers. "Was it something you loved or something you were made to do?"

I grabbed a vase and put the flowers in water, breathing in their glorious scent. "I wasn't forced, but it was pretty much expected. My dad and brothers all played. I liked it and I was pretty good. But it wasn't something I wanted to devote my life to. I stopped after high school. I wasn't ready to deal with being an openly gay player on a college team—it was difficult as it was being a closeted player on a high school team, only my parents knew at that time and they forbid me to speak of it." I placed the flowers on the kitchen table, loving how easily they brightened up the room.

"My dad was angry I had no interest or skill in sports— yet if I tried to please him by going out for something sports related, he berated me for being stupid enough to try." Charlie sighed. "Okay, I think we can agree our parents sucked. Moving on to happier subjects. Coffee?"

"Yes, please." We spent a few moments playing with the cats and then headed toward Piping Hot.

While we walked Charlie got a text.

"Shit," he said, stopping in the middle of the sidewalk.

"What?" My stomach plummeted.

"Jo Ellen wants us to meet her and Harley. Says she has information."

"The shop or her place?"

"I'll ask, but either way, we need coffee." Charlie thumbed in a reply.

I took his hand. "We've got this. We'll get the information and make a plan. We can't make a plan without info. Let's see what she's found out."

"Agreed." Charlie squeezed my hand. "And once this is all

sorted, no matter how it turns out, we need a getaway. I don't care where we go, we just need a break."

"I'm down."

We arrived at Piping Hot and Charlie took a deep breath as he checked his texts.

"She's here." He gave me a weak smile. "Here goes nothing."

THIRTEEN

CHARLIE

NIX and I settled in at the most secluded back table in the corner with Jo and Harley. Everyone had coffee and breakfast sandwiches. I'd also gotten a cinnamon roll for Nix and I to share.

"Good morning," Jo said. "What perfect timing we've got, huh?"

"This place seems to have it in spades," I said with a wink toward Nix. "I'm almost afraid to ask what you know."

Harley chuckled. "She's better than a detective, let me tell you. I think you'll be pleased."

Jo Ellen launched into an animated and highly opinionated explanation of what she and the lawyers had been able to surmise from the situation over the last several days. "I want to start with the fact that Stephen will *not* be purchasing Wayne's nor will he be pestering you about it ever again. I'd like to get that out of the way so you're not on the edge of hyperventilating while you wait for me to get to that part."

I smiled as relief washed over me. "Thanks. I appreciate that."

"So, there's a reason Stephen waited until Charlie owned the place before showing up." Jo leaned in as she spoke. "He'd been after his grandfather for *years* about buying the store and Wayne was adamant he would *not* sell to Stephen. So adamant, in fact, Wayne has it in his will *and* on file with his attorney that his grandson—or any individual involved with his grandson's business dealings—will *never* be allowed to purchase the store. Stephen knew he couldn't buy from Wayne, so he waited until Charlie was the owner."

Anger bubbled through me. "So, he just waited and then tried to bully me into selling?"

"Basically," Harley said with a scowl. "Wayne always said the kid was a mean one."

"But can't he still contest the sale? Keep bothering Charlie to sell?" Nix asked.

"Hang on, I'll get to that." Jo sipped her coffee. "Hanson and Kane spoke to Wayne's attorney—they opted at this point not to involve Wayne since he's got so much going on and he'd likely feel the need to drive all the way back up here —turns out, this thing between Wayne and Stephen goes even deeper. I guess Stephen threatened Wayne a few years back. Told him he'd come after him with claims of Wayne being mentally incompetent, use whatever problems he could stir up to get Wayne to sell."

"Damn, what an asshole," I muttered.

"Right." Jo nodded. "So, Wayne took a preemptive stance and had a full assessment of his mental state completed. Clearly, he's competent. His lawyer has the results in Wayne's file in case Stephen would ever follow through on the threat."

"What does that have to do with Charlie, though?" Nix asked.

"Maybe nothing, but it's part of the story. However, *if* Stephen opted to contest the sale and Wayne still wouldn't

budge, I guess he could play the mental incompetence card—
I don't think Stephen knows Wayne had the tests done." Jo
took another drink of coffee. "Anyway, Hanson and Kane also
got in contact with Stephen, but he refused to speak to them
—probably to his detriment—so they went to his attorney.
Come to find out, there have been *several* complaints made
against Stephen and his company over the past few years—
unfair and bordering on illegal business practices. Seems the
attorney may be a bit fed-up; he spoke candidly of multiple
issues Stephen has had recently with not only the state and
several counties, but also that he's in hot water with the
Better Business Bureau." Jo smirked and shrugged. "Kane
decided to drop a tidbit of information into the conversation
and let the attorney know the good folks of Briarton have
drafted a complaint to the county, the state, and the BBB.
Come to find out, if one more complaint is filed, Stephen will
face several very high fines *and* be at risk of losing one or
more of his permits."

"So, that's it? He's just going to back off?" I asked, not
sure whether to believe it was that easy.

"Appears so. His attorney says he's got quite a bit of dirt
on Stephen—enough that the kid can't fire him if he
doesn't want to risk all the shit getting out and coming
back to bite him. Sounds like both the attorney and Stephen
are pretty shifty and basically held together by what dirt
they have on each other. Super business practice." Jo rolled
her eyes. "So, Stephen likely won't quit his scumbag ways
of doing business, but he'll leave Briarton alone." Jo
beamed proudly.

"So, Wayne's is still Charlie's? No big legal battle? No
more worrying?" Nix asked as he grabbed my hand.

"I guess we can't know one hundred percent—Stephen
could always go rogue and cause problems—but his attorney
seems to think he'll move on to acquiring businesses in areas

where he won't get so much pushback. If only to save himself from more reports filed against him."

Morgan and Justin walked over during a lull in the breakfast rush.

"I see smiles and relaxed postures," Justin said. "Tell me this means good news."

"Good news," I announced, unable to wipe the huge smile from my face.

"Excellent," Morgan said with a slap on my back. He handed Nix his phone and medical bag. "Bart's daughter brought these in last night. Said she wasn't sure the best place to drop them off, but knew we were friends. Told me to tell you how sorry she is about Bart and the cow."

Nix laughed and brushed fingers over his stitches. "Bart was a pain, but the cow was worse."

We all chatted while finishing our food and coffee. Morgan and Justin had to get back to work, but they invited us to come to dinner soon.

Harley cleared his throat. "Change of subject, but I wanted to ask about Otto. When I went to visit the other day, I was able to coerce him into taking a walk with me."

"That's a feat in and of itself," I said.

"I know. I'll take it when I can get it." Harley smiled. "But I noticed he struggled a bit more than usual with the front steps. His gait is good most of the time—*really* good for his age—but the steps seem to be getting more difficult."

I rubbed my forehead. "I've been meaning to look into putting in a ramp. Leaving the steps, but adding a ramp either beside or over to the side."

"Let's do it," Nix said, clapping his hands together. "Between YouTube and all of us, I'm sure we can figure something out. It will be a nice little project. Otto can sit on the porch and boss us around."

We all laughed.

Looked like we had a ramp to build.

Nearly a month later, our little group sat on Otto's porch sipping tea and lemonade as we admired our handy-work on the ramp.

It had taken quite a bit of time to watch videos, buy materials, and find a day everyone was available, but once we started the project early one Saturday morning, we were done by mid-afternoon.

"Looks good," Otto declared. "We did a great job."

I snorted. "Yeah, wouldn't have been able to finish without your bossy ass making suggestions and telling us what we were doing wrong."

"You're welcome," my uncle said with a smile.

The past several weeks had flown by in a whirlwind of doctor appointments, prescriptions, therapy, edits, writing, and spending time at Wayne's.

The medication was pretty much back to regulating my anxiety and depression, and my therapy appointments were going well.

Wayne's was running great and I fell a little more in love with the place every moment I spent there. My business allowed the folks in Briarton to get their needs and wants met while never having to leave town to find some unfriendly discount supply store—plus, we had the best options when it came to handmade, homegrown, fresh, and local.

My writing was back in a groove. I'd always been one for a schedule and I realized the words had suffered just as much as my mental state when the medication and therapy slipped. I was back on a schedule with daily time carved out for edits, my own writing, and ghostwriting.

Nix and I were amazing. We'd introduced the cats and

they dealt with it about as good as you'd think four adult cats would. Cheddar and CoJack didn't *love* Cricket and Hopper—and the feeling was mutual—but they tolerated each other's presence when Nix and I wanted to spend multiple days together without needing to run home and take care of food and litter boxes.

We hadn't slept apart since the cow-hoof-to-the-head incident and, if I had my way, we never would. We'd fallen into an easy routine of staying at my house during the week so I had my office for writing. Most weekends were spent at Nix's. The cats pretty much just rolled with the weekly changes in location.

Morgan and Justin had invited us to spend a weekend with them at their cabin. We were planning it for a time farther into the fall when the leaves were changing and the weather cooler—it was also going to take Morgan that long to convince Justin to leave Piping Hot for three days.

I understood Justin's worries. Even though I knew Wayne's could run without me for days and weeks at a time, I still didn't like the thought of leaving. But I'd promised Nix I'd get my writing caught up and even get word counts ahead *and* make sure my employees knew I was gonna be gone.

It wasn't like Nix was all that much better. He fretted about leaving his patients, but the new home health nurse Dr. Pierce had hired was really good and had already agreed to cover Nix's appointments while we were gone.

Overall, life was good.

Had I known way back when I was miserable and lonely in the city that moving to a small town with my uncle would bring me so much happiness and fulfillment, I probably wouldn't have believed it. Or I would have packed up and moved in hopes of escaping the turmoil.

I shook my head as I took in the people on Otto's front porch—Harley, Jo Ellen, Morgan, Justin, Nix, my uncle—and smiled. Trying to force what I'd found wouldn't have worked. I had to have patience and wait on fate's perfect timing.

"You expecting someone?" Otto asked, breaking me from my happy little thoughts.

Nix came to stand next to me as I looked toward the driveway where a car was pulling in.

"No. You?" I asked.

"I have a date coming over later, but not right now," Otto said, squinting toward the drive. "Well, I'll be damned."

I glanced again toward the unfamiliar car and gasped.

Nix turned to me, concerned. "You okay? Who is it?"

As the woman walked toward me with a huge smile, I rushed down the steps and ran toward her.

"Oh my God, what are you doing here?" I asked as I lifted Stella into a huge hug and spun her around. "How long can you stay? You're staying with me, right?"

Stella laughed and returned my hug. "I'm here for about a week and you're damned right I'm staying with you."

I settled her feet back on the ground and stared at my best friend. "You look amazing. Overseas seems to agree with you."

"Falling in love and having fabulous sex agrees with me," Stella said with a wink. "You look pretty damn good yourself. Small-town living?"

My cheeks pinked and I bit my lip, throwing a glance over my shoulder toward Nix. "In addition to falling in love and fabulous sex," I mumbled.

Stella laughed. "I know, right?!"

"Come on, meet the crew." I took her hand and led her to the front porch to make introductions.

Morgan and Justin gave friendly hellos before heading back to the shop with promises to get together before Stella left.

Harley and Jo chatted for a bit before taking their leave, assuring Stella they'd see her at Piping Hot the next day.

"What made you want to come back?" Otto asked. He'd always been fond of Stella.

"Well, I'd heard so many amazing things about Nixon, I started planning a trip almost right away—like, God guys, couldn't you do the whole slow-burn, simmering relationship thing and give a girl some time to plan visits? Oh no, you two had to go falling head-over-heels in like twenty-four hours, forcing your girl here on a plane at the first possible moment." Stella grinned, her eyes sparkling as she studied Nix and me. "Don't get me wrong, I waited for a good deal, but I *did* start searching from the first time Charlie told me about the love of his life."

I left the three to chat while I grabbed Stella a glass of ice for lemonade. When I returned, I swore my best friend and boyfriend had already bonded for life. For the next couple hours, I watched them in amazement as they chatted away, never once making me feel left out, and acted as if they'd been best friends for life.

"Seriously, I think it's something with you," I said to Nix. "You swore you'd never fallen for someone as quickly as you fell for me."

"Yeah?" he chuckled and kissed me.

"And then Stell shows up and you're best friends within moments. I thought I was your special, unique, immediate-connection person." I pretended to pout.

"Don't blame him," Stella said. "You know I'm fabulous and people can't help but be drawn to me."

I smiled. "It's true. You're like a damn magnet."

"Just be glad we like each other," Nix said. "It would be really awkward to have to declare war and fight your best friend over you."

"Awww, you'd fight for me?" I teased. "I feel so loved."

"I'd fight back," Stella said. "But..."

I gasped, pretending to be offended. "What? You wouldn't fight to the death for me? Avenge my honor?"

"Wellllll," she drawled, a grin teasing her face. "I kinda *have* to get back in one piece."

I narrowed my eyes. I'd known her too long to let the moment pass. "You've got a secret. What is it?"

"I'm getting married. Odette asked me right before I left —said it was her insurance to make sure I came back to her." Stella slipped a ring from her pocket and put it on.

"Oh my God." I grabbed her hand. "That's gorgeous. When is the wedding?"

"Next year," Stella said. "That gives you plenty of time, right? You'll be there?"

"Hell yes, we'll be there. Wait, where is there?"

"France. It's where she lives—in this great little city—and I've all but moved in with her." Stella glanced at Nix. "You'll make sure he's there, right?"

"Obviously. Who isn't going to make sure a trip to France happens?"

Over the next week, I couldn't wipe the grin from my face as my best friend and new friends bonded. Stella and I fell right back into the special relationship we'd always had. It was something special to watch two of the most important people in my life realize just why I loved the other one so damn much.

Tears flowed on the day Stella had to leave. She all but demanded a blood oath promise we'd be in France for her wedding. I had a feeling the three of us would be chatting on video calls a lot over the next several months.

Later that night, Nix held me after we made love. "You okay?"

"Gonna be sore tomorrow, but yeah, I'm good."

He snorted. "Good to know, but I meant with Stella gone.

I know you've missed her and it seems like we didn't get to have her here for very long."

My heart was a big pile of goo in my still-heaving chest. "Awww, I love you. Thank you so much for loving my friend. It hadn't been something I'd given much thought to—I love you both so much, I just assumed you'd love each other—but it would have been super awkward if there was tension."

"You did a good job picking your best friend, she's great." Nix kissed the top of my head. "I love you."

I sighed, cuddling into him. "A trip to the cabin in a month. A trip to France to watch my best friend get married next year. With luck, a new ghostwriting contract *and* finishing this romantic comedy. And Wayne's starts carrying local soaps, lotions, and candles next week. Up until now, I didn't even know it was possible to feel this happy and content."

Nix hummed. "Do you still get sad sometimes that we met so much later in life?"

I thought about that for a moment and shook my head. "No, I think I've realized I was nowhere close to being ready for a relationship before now. I *wanted* one, but I wasn't ready. Who knows, if I had met you fifteen or twenty years ago, maybe neither of us would have been at a point in our lives where our instant connection could have happened." I nuzzled my nose against his soft chest hair. "I think we met at exactly the right moment."

"Perfect timing," Nix murmured, tipping my chin up to brush a slow, sweet kiss over my lips.

"Absolutely perfect," I agreed, melting into his kiss.

EPILOGUE

NIX

One Year Later

"If you keep that up, we'll have to rush to get to the airport," I said, groaning as Charlie sucked my cock deep to the back of his throat.

"We have time. Quickie then a shower. Everything is already packed. Morgan drives fast anyway." Charlie continued working over my throbbing morning erection.

"Fine, but I wanna be in you if I'm coming," I groused and pushed him to his back. Shifting to tease my tongue over Charlie's hole, I grabbed blindly for the lube as I worked him open.

Charlie gasped and writhed under me. "Please, Nix, I'm ready. Don't wanna be late."

I chuckled as I slicked myself and pressed into him. "Greedy little thing, never afraid to use a situation to your advantage."

Charlie groaned as I slid deep. "I do what needs to be done."

We settled into a slow, hard rhythm, the scent and sound of our sex permeating the room.

"Last time fucking you in this room," I said with a thrust that made Charlie grunt.

"Make it good," he answered, pulling me down to devour my lips with his.

We'd decided a few months ago to move in together. It made the most sense to sell my place and keep Charlie's since Otto had the perfect set-up. We knew the older man would possibly not be able to live on his own until the end, but I had no concerns about his current safety.

When we returned from our trip to France to watch Stella get married, we'd move all of my stuff into Charlie's and put my house on the market. Jo Ellen had already hinted she knew of several people ready to jump at the chance to buy my place.

Charlie whimpered under me as I pounded hard and slow into his tight, hot hole. "Please, I'm so close."

"Jerk yourself," I demanded as I increased my speed.

When Charlie's release shot between us and his ass gripped my cock, I gave in and let my orgasm roll through me as I spilled my hot, sticky seed into him.

Less than an hour later, hair still wet from the fastest showers we'd ever taken, we threw our luggage into Morgan's Jeep and thanked Justin profusely for the coffees he handed us. The fit was tight with all four of us and our luggage, but Stella had promised we could do laundry at her place and she'd have all the toiletries we could possibly need, so we'd packed as light as possible for the overseas flight.

Morgan and Justin walked with us into the airport as far as they were allowed to go.

"Thank you so much for the ride and for watching the cats and checking in on Otto," Charlie said, giving both men a hug.

"Not a problem, just promise you'll come back. We'd be lonely if you guys ever decided to move away," Justin said.

"No way, Briarton is home," I said. "We've got *one* house to sell, no way we want to deal with selling two."

"Plus, a Briarton wedding in the spring would be amazing," Justin said with a grin. He'd been teasing us about making things official for months.

"Justin," Morgan warned.

"Just because you guys had *two* weddings in Briarton doesn't mean we have to have one," I said, throwing a glance toward Charlie to see if I could get a read on him. Any talk of a weddings lately seemed to spook him.

Charlie caught my eye and shrugged. "I don't know, we've got a great backyard for an outdoor wedding, and spring in Briarton *is* beautiful." He winked at a beaming Justin and leaned in to kiss my cheek. "I'm not ready to veto fall either. Maybe we'll get inspiration while we're away."

"We are totally talking colors and food when you get back," Justin exclaimed.

"I'm down," Charlie answered. He threw a look my way. "If this one is."

I wrapped my arm around his neck. "I'll buy a damn ring and propose right here if that's what you want." I kissed him, hard and fast. "I'm down. One hundred percent down." We had the vows we'd whispered in our dark bedroom, but I would happily put a ring on the man's hand. In a heartbeat.

We eventually made our way to the loading area, hand-in-hand, and I couldn't help but think this trip was yet one more of those *first day of the rest of your life* type things and I couldn't wait to see what the future held for Charlie and me.

The End

If you enjoyed this story, be sure to read The Perfect Blend if you haven't already.

Like A.D. Ellis's work? Check it out on Amazon and in KindleUnlimited.

In the next few pages, you'll find other titles by A.D. Ellis. Take a look and see what strikes your fancy. Be sure to follow and like on social media and sign up for the newsletter. If you're not in the Ellis Elite Facebook group, we'd love to have you!

Note about demisexuality: First, and foremost, the term demisexual can mean different things for different people. Charlie is a unique individual, just like the rest of us, and the way demisexuality works for him may not be the way it works for others.

For more information regarding demisexuality, please see the articles HERE and HERE.

If you don't have time to check the articles, I pulled out a couple quotes I think are helpful (but I'd still encourage you to read and learn for yourself).

"Demisexuality is a sexual orientation where people only experience sexual attraction to folks that they have close emotional connections with."

"Again, every person is unique, and what one demisexual person enjoys might not be what another person enjoys."

ALSO BY A.D. ELLIS

The Perfect Blend- A steamy, M/M age-gap, marriage of convenience, coffee shop romance

Adore (Remington Place 1) is a steamy, age-gap, bi-awakening, dad's best friend M/M romance with a sassy smartass and a sexy silver fox. It's the first book in the Remington Place series and can be read as a stand-alone.

Crave (Remington Place 2) is a steamy, friends-to-lovers, fake relationship M/M romance with a virgin nursing student and a gruff, grumbly construction worker.

Desire (Remington Place 3) is a steamy, age-gap, hurt/comfort M/M romance featuring a heart-of-gold mechanic and a twink who's a lot stronger than he realizes. *Please note: This story has mention of sex trafficking and sexual abuse.*

Yearn (Remington Place 4)- a steamy, enemies-to-lovers, forced proximity M/M romance between two EMS workers who have hated each other for a decade.

Power Struggle is a steamy M/M, age-gap, forced proximity romance set in a small town. A twenty-year history, rival schools and jobs, and a hotel with only one bed make for a hot and heavy, sweet and sexy, HEA-guaranteed love story.

Take Me Home M/M age-gap, opposites-attract romance with plenty of steam and a scene that will make you appreciate camouflage and work boots

Let Love In M/M age-gap, forced proximity, dad's best friend, bisexual-awakening romance. Available on AUDIO!

Let Love Win M/M brother's best friend romance. Available on AUDIO!

Buried Secrets Romantic suspense stand-alone title. Available on AUDIO!

Silver in the City (3 books- meet the Silver crew you read about in Forged in the City) Available on AUDIO!

Forged in the City (3 books- a spin-off series from Silver in the City) Available on AUDIO

The BJ Boys Series (3 books, small town, big love) Available on AUDIO

Forever Better Together (friends to lovers) Available on AUDIO!

His Reluctant Cowboy (age gap, opposites attract, cowboy romance) Available on AUDIO!

What Blooms Beneath (LGBT Fantasy romance) Available on AUDIO!

Sawyer

(this was the first M/M I wrote and you may remember Sawyer and Luke being mentioned in Barrett & Ivan as well as in Ryker & Gavin)

Plus several other titles:

Saving Us

Stranded Hearts (a short story)

Escape (a 3-book collection of fun stories)

A.D.'s first stories (all male/female except Sawyer which is male/male) are in the Torey Hope and Torey Hope: The Later Years series. Find the 8 book box set HERE or you can find each individual title on Amazon.

For Nicky

Because of Beckett

Christmas in Torey Hope

Loving Josie

Decker

Sawyer

Zach

Kendrick

ACKNOWLEDGMENTS

It's always so hard to write this part because I'm worried I'll forget someone without meaning to.

Readers- you are the reason I write. As long as you continue reading my stories, I'll continue writing them. Thank you for your support.

Bloggers- your support, reviews, and promotion are very much appreciated. Thank you!

My author buddies- I don't know that I could keep doing this without our brainstorm sessions, laughter, road trips, meals, wine, and friendship as my support.

Thank you to my alpha readers, betas, editors, proofreaders, and ARC readers! Your eyes and input are beyond important to me.

Brett and Gage- as usual, I doubt you even grasp how much your support, input, and friendship mean to me. This author journey has brought many wonderful things into my life, and you both are two of the BEST! I'm blessed to call you friends.

My family and friends- thank you for your love and support, always.

ABOUT THE AUTHOR

A.D. Ellis is an Indiana girl, born and raised. She spends much of her time in central Indiana as a teacher in the inner city of Indianapolis, being a mom to two amazing teens, and wondering how she and her husband of over two decades have managed to not drive each other insane. A lot of her time is also devoted to phone call avoidance and her hatred of cooking.

She loves chocolate, wine, pizza, and naps along with reading and writing romance. These loves don't leave much time for housework, much to the chagrin of her husband. Who would pick cleaning the house over a nap or a good book? She uses any extra time to increase her fluency in sarcasm.

Sign up at http://www.subscribepage.com/ADEllisNewsMMRomance for a FREE male/male romance book.

Find all of my books at Amazon- https://www.amazon.com/A.D.-Ellis/e/B00K0YJ8CW

Follow my website http://www.adellisauthor.com or find me on Facebook

http://www.facebook.com/adellisauthor

Check out my TikTok- https://www.tiktok.com/@adellisauthor

You can also find me on Twitter http://www.twitter.com/ADEllisAuthor